THE WHITE REVIEW

22

C000004999

Urs Fischer
soft
08 June – 18 August 2018

Sadie Coles HQ
62 Kingly Street
London W1B 5QN

Sarah Sze

Victoria Miro

8 JUNE – 28 JULY 2018

16 WHARF ROAD · LONDON N1 7RW

Images in Debris, 2018

Image: Dinu Li, *Nation Family*, 2017, video still (detail)

DINU LI
The Anatomy of Place

23 June - 14 July 2018

DANIELLE ARNAUD
123 Kennington Road, London SE11 6SF
www.daniellearnaud.com

ARTS COUNCIL ENGLAND

Supported using public funding by
ARTS COUNCIL
ENGLAND

Metal

Austin Austin

Certified Organic Bodycare

austinaustinorganic.com

ARCADE

87 Lever Street
London EC1V 3RA
+44 (0)20 7683 2999
info@thisisarcade.art
www.thisisarcade.art
@thisisArcade

Published by The White Review, June 2018
Edition of 1,800

Printed by Unicum, Tilburg
Typeset in Nouveau Blanche

ISBN No. 978-0-9957437-4-8

The White Review is a registered charity (number 1148690)

The White Review, 243 Knightsbridge, London SW7 1DN
www.thewhitereview.org

Supported using public funding by
ARTS COUNCIL ENGLAND
LOTTERY FUNDED

EDITORIAL

In her interview with the novelist Jenny Offill, Hannah Rosefield encounters Offill in the process of writing her new novel. Meeting a novelist at such a point is rare: we're used to reading a writer discussing a finished book rather than one that is still being written. Offill describes how recent political events have caused her to change, edit and update her work-in-progress, explaining: 'I'm trying to figure out how a bookish person would try to engage with this moment in time.'

The White Review has always been a testing-ground for new work and ideas, and this issue in particular seems to catch a moment of change and sheer eventfulness, and captures writers and artists thinking through how we might respond to these times. Earlier this year, a fourteen-day strike was staged by university staff and students against cuts to pensions. Our roundtable on the university took place just after the end of the strike, and in a conversation that ranged over marketisation, workers' rights and campus sexual harassment participants took the opportunity to reflect, discuss and debate, and to articulate thoughts-in-progress about the future of the modern university.

The idea of a multi-vocal response is not alien to Kerstin Brätsch, whose belief in community, and that many hands make a painting, is discussed in an interview with this distinctive artist, followed by a selection of her ecstatic, vibrant works. Following on from their electrifying performances in the UK at the start of the year, we're delighted to feature an interview with poet Danez Smith, one of the most exciting new voices to emerge during a particularly fertile period in contemporary poetry.

We're pleased to publish a portfolio of poems by Lucy Mercer, the winner of our inaugural poetry prize, which was specifically created to recognise works-in-progress, and support poets working on their first collections. The judges praised this burgeoning collection for its philosophical enquiry and range of formal experimentation in 'poems that spoke to each other' with sureness and authority. Alongside this is fiction by Maria Hummer, which explores love in a virtual reality world, and the strange and disturbing 'Reunion' by Vera Giaconi, translated by Megan McDowell. 'Sea Monsters' by Chloe Aridjis is the story of a young runaway to a Mexico beach in search of a troupe of Ukrainian dwarves. In this extract from a longer work, we see the beginnings of a novel taking shape.

Julia Bell's essay 'Really Techno' explores the possibilities for freedom and discovery in a Berlin nightclub, while Scholastique Mukasonga traces the Rukarara river, both as a memory and a symbol, and in the physical path it takes through the landscape where she was born. Finally, Quinn Latimer begins to see and read women on fire everywhere, and in her luminous piece she thinks through what this dramatic image and metaphor might tell us about our present moment.

ON UNIVERSITIES ROUNDTABLE

What is a university for? Even for those outside of higher education, this is a question that's becoming increasingly difficult to avoid. In February and March this year, the Universities and Colleges Union (UCU) organised fourteen days of strike action over a four-week period, which saw staff and students standing on picket lines in freezing weather conditions, mass marches and rallies through campuses and city centres, and a significant rise in union membership across the UK. Primarily, the strike was about pensions, but it soon became apparent that for many participants the industrial action was a form of resistance against the encroaching neoliberal agenda for higher education. Banners on the picket line borrowed from Mark Fisher: 'Against the slow cancellation of the future'.

The pensions issue itself – the proposal from Universities UK (UUK) to transform the Universities Superannuation Scheme (USS) from a defined benefit scheme to a defined contribution scheme – is symptomatic of the increasing financialisation of the university. The former guarantees its members a retirement income; the latter pegs returns to the stock market, and threatens staff with a loss of between 10 and 40 per cent in their retirement income. UUK, which describes itself as 'the voice of universities', is an organisation of the vice-chancellors or principals of higher education institutions, who have seen their own pay more than quadruple in less than twenty years. Meanwhile, staff pay has seen a real-term decline of 21 per cent since 2009. Defined benefit pensions are deferred wages; the proposed changes provided proof, if proof were needed, of the political agenda behind the current drive to reform British universities.

This discussion took place just after the vote to suspend strike action was passed, and inevitably, we had a lot to discuss. Alongside the more visible scandals of the past few years – Toby Young's appointment to the Office for Students springs immediately to mind, and the ongoing right wing media attack on campus no-platform policies – most university staff are increasingly on some variation of an insecure contract, something that actively works against the diversification of the academic workplace. The Home Office crackdown on student visas and the introduction of the controversial Prevent Duty, which in practice consistently targets Muslim and BME students, raises serious questions about the duty of care owed to students by university management. The removal of the cap on tuition fees, the abolition of maintenance grants and the establishment of the REF and TEF – the Research and Teaching Excellence Frameworks, respectively, which rank institutions' output in order to justify 'better' universities charging higher fees – place an ever-increasing emphasis on value for money, and transform students into consumers.

Something we returned to several times during our discussion was how best to recognise that students and staff, despite attempts to pit them against each other, are being harmed by the same system. Teaching and administrative staff striking together provided a visible reminder of the other kinds of work universities rely on, something often overlooked in coverage of the dispute. Academics have traditionally been reluctant to conceive of themselves as workers; the working to contract implemented on non-strike days forced some staff to redefine their relationship to labour. Our conversation dwelt for a long time on notions of 'sacrifice' and 'vocation': if universities rely upon unwaged labour and 'goodwill', how can staff resist? And how can we stop ourselves passing on bad habits to students by setting a self-renouncing example? The current government believes departments should be ranked on their graduates' future earning potential: how can we help students grapple with their economic anxieties whilst simultaneously rejecting this co-option of education by market forces?

My own position, both in the context of the strikes and in academia as a whole, is marginal: I'm both a student and a worker, splitting my time – and, it sometimes feels like, my allegiances– between writing my PhD thesis and supervising undergraduates. A common feeling amongst others I've spoken to in this position was of a heightening of precarity: an awareness, even in the midst of uplifting solidarity on the picket line, that you weren't quite a colleague, and that the idea that you might one day have a secure contract, let alone a pension, feels dangerously hopeful. The turbulence of the past few months has both provided a sense of optimism that another university might be possible – a collective social good, accessible to all – and revealed the extent of the systematic and structural change that needs to happen in order to fulfil that promise.   HELEN CHARMAN

HELEN CHARMAN   In the aftermath of the strike, do you feel at all optimistic about the situation facing universities in the UK?

MATTHEW BEAUMONT   One of the crises for higher education in the last twenty or thirty years has been in governance: the increasingly corporate managerial structures and the marginalisation both of academics as administrators and of democratically accountable forms of governance. So one of the things I found really encouraging about the strike was the solidarity, the collegiality... It seemed to me there was something very hopeful to be excavated from the way in which striking colleagues related to each other, for the most part, certainly in my institution, in a non-judgemental, non-vindictive way, to non-striking colleagues as well as amongst themselves. I think that momentum has to be continued, that momentum has to be pushed through, whatever else happens, whether there are further strikes and industrial action over pensions, over pay, whatever...

VAHNI CAPILDEO   I'm by no means an expert, partly because being on short-term contracts and not always in academia, this has been the first time I have taken part in a protest action in the UK rather than in the Global South. I don't really see the strike as being over. I mean, this particular strike has been called off, and there has been a sort of de-subscribing from email lists, etcetera, but there is an awakening of interest amongst persons both sympathetic and not sympathetic to the view of education as a good in itself. I think awakening of interest is bound to be a thing – both a good and a bad thing. I suppose the third point I would make, which is a little bit fussy and anecdotal, is that I didn't really experience solidarity at the picket lines. I experienced quite extraordinary levels of direct racism and sexism such as I haven't been used to.

BEAUMONT   Christ.

WASEEM YAQOOB   That is really shocking.

CAPILDEO   I don't think it is shocking, it is normal.

BEAUMONT   From fellow strikers or from people passing the picket line or passing through the picket line?

CAPILDEO   From fellow strikers.

CHARMAN   I had a few sexist comments from people crossing the picket line.

YAQOOB   We had to issue instructions to our pickets not to heckle people passing through, and some of the things said were sexist. So obviously things that happen in the everyday were happening on the picket lines too.

I suppose one of the hopeful things I found about the strikes is that there's been a lot of discontent for as long as I've been at the university, which isn't very long, but long enough to remember when the higher education reforms to marketise the sector came in. One of the frustrations of organising as a union organiser was a sense that there weren't many types of action that would be appropriate to bring lots of things to the forefront of whatever struggles were going on: marketisation, racism, sexual harassment and so on. One of the frustrations was the sense that a strike over something that's strictly about pay or benefits wouldn't really bring all of these struggles together. And I think what was really great about this dispute was that it took the lid off – it let lots of people come out through teach-outs, through conversations on the picket line, and organise on lots and lots of different fronts. I hope the legacy of that can continue. But as Vahni said, it also brought out lots of fractures and conflicts along racial and sexual and gender lines that were already there, and unions have always had problems with these things, so there is a lot of work to do.

The second thing I would say is, no. I'm not that hopeful because one of the significant battles has been about reform across the whole sector – competition, marketisation. The Office of Students was finally set up late last year and we can see in that how the government has an authoritarian, market-based vision for universities. It's not clear to me how strike action in its traditional form is going to repel those attacks. We need to find new ways of resisting.

BEAUMONT   I'm not excessively sanguine about the future, but one of the great strengths of the strike was that it wasn't a narrowly economic one, in terms of its issues. It was very political, and the conversations and debates that happened on the picket line, among both strikers and non-striking colleagues, were highly politicised. They weren't just about the marketisation, monetisation and privatisation of higher education, but about the neoliberal dispensation more broadly. Of course, there's only grounds for political optimism if our struggle is tied into a broader political movement – one that attempts systematically to unite generations, to unite across class, race, gender divisions, in a struggle against austerity and the economic regime that underpins them. To unite against the devastating attack on the public sector, on the very notion of the public, that has taken place in the forty years since Margaret Thatcher came to power.

'I'M OKAY'

CAPILDEO   There wasn't actually a huge amount of debate with the students who I encountered on the picket line. There were very very many crossing the picket line to go to university. They refused leaflets with what I thought, speaking as a poet rather than as a very recent union member, was an interesting phrase: 'I'm okay.' Of course it's a colloquialism, but it was interesting because on the one hand there is a culture of sensitivity, where a student might complain if an individual person is under attack, but there is also a culture of being armoured. This idea that you are okay, that you can't bear to question the fundamental principles around which your existence is organised, because by doing so you might have to admit to a lack of control.

BEAUMONT   You're right. That's an interesting symptomatic response, not least as symptomatic of the well-documented transformation of students into consumers and customers. 'I'm okay' is the kind of thing a customer says when they're offered a free iced latte when they go past a Costa or something – it's a consumer response.

CAPILDEO   It is, but it is also a kind of abused child response: 'I'm okay, I'm only being beaten, I'm not being starved.' Obviously they're not okay, they're being overcharged fees, fed franchised food which is unhealthy, made to pay rent for accommodation which is unaffordable, sent out with debt, taught by precarious over-stressed people who have not worked long enough to build up security in their expertise. I started asking questions like, 'Do you know what your fees are paying for? Do you know how much your lecturers earn? Do you know how much your vice-chancellor earns?' And when I asked these questions some just looked stricken and suddenly very young. The majority didn't know what their fees paid for.

YAQOOB   There's also a sense in which some of the bodies, in particular student unions, that were previously relied upon to push back against fees, to push back against consumerisation, are now becoming part of the managerial structure. So some of the conduits around which staff and student solidarity used to be built can no longer

necessarily be relied upon. Actually the model that student unions are being pushed into in a lot of places is that of a sort of welfare provider. They're there to pick up the pieces of the strain and the stress of being in debt-funded higher education knowing that you're going into a terrible job market. So there are wider issues at play. Sorry to be bleak.

BEAUMONT   I don't want to be Pollyannaish, but I was deeply gratified in my department by the levels of solidarity from students and by their willingness to understand. I think there was a certain amount of suspicion and scepticism and even ignorance regarding the issues that were being fought over, and their political implications and the ways in which they might interact and intersect with their own interests. But that was until we held a meeting for everyone in the department who wanted to attend. All those proposing to take strike action explained themselves, and tried to make themselves accountable to the students. And a real dialogue began, which continued throughout the duration of the strike. Ultimately, I found the students' appetite for connecting up their disappointments and disillusionments with ours was impressive and quite poignant.

CAPILDEO   I suppose that if the students had been hurt by the continuation of the strike into an exam period then that would have been correct, because strike action is a very particular type of action and this strike was dependent on the acceptance of the commercialisation of the relationship between academic and student, and the point of the strike is to hurt the consumer. Whereas if one were to analyse the university as treating the student as the product rather than as the consumer, then that would be different.

CONSUMER AND PRODUCT; REFUNDS; DEBT

CAPILDEO   There's an incoherence in wanting the students to be both consumer and product, to show solidarity with the strike and be hurt by the strike. It's not really possible. So how appropriate is the traditional form of strike action? Oddly, I did appreciate something my teaching colleagues were not so happy about: the length of the strike. And the reason I was happy about it was that academics in disciplines more 'real world' than mine – economists, journalists, lawyers – were doing proper serious research into the strike. The longer the strike went on the more there were extraordinary discoveries and documentation being produced.

YAQOOB   I want to go back to the student thing, to what you were saying about industrial action. I don't think you were being Pollyannaish. I speak today as some of our students have blockaded the finance office of the university on the issue of fossil fuel divestment. And throughout the strike for a large part the student body were at the leading edge, they were leading the debate about the future of the university and the academics, my colleagues, were catching up. They led an occupation with extraordinarily precise and clever and strategic demands and they got what they wanted from the university and that was extraordinary to see. So I just want to strike a note of hope. But on the industrial action, I do think the spectre of hitting exams put union organisers in a difficult place, because on the one hand you want students to go into exam term onside with the strike, supportive, making us feel good about picketing. On the other hand, we also want them to complain in a certain way, in a way that management doesn't think is coordinated by us but is actually a sign of genuine anger. The possibility of refunds was in there as well. Of course in the context of a standard industrial dispute demands for large-scale refunds would be incredibly disruptive. And time and time again we were asked as a union branch whether we were comfortable with requests for refunds. I thought it wasn't our place to tell students how to express their anger, but on the other hand there are some serious issues with acting as if you're already a consumer.

CHARMAN   I teach for the postgraduate outreach programme, and over the seven years I've been involved in access and outreach work I've noticed a definite change in the questions students ask me. At GCSE level or even younger, the questions now are all about whether they will get a job after university. What kind of job will they get if they do a humanities degree? And I never know what to say because I can't lie. That's not ethical. But I disagree completely with the idea that the purpose of university is to get a job, that knowledge should be instrumentalised. But they are in a double bind as students. They can't not be under those pressures, they can't not be worried about graduating with a huge amount of debt and then trying to find a job. So I worry about students when it comes to the issue of whether they are the consumer or the product. It's very very hard

for them whilst they are under that pressure to actually work out what it is they can be, let alone what they want to be.

CAPILDEO   Of course.

BEAUMONT   I agree: it's very difficult to know what to say in response to that. The issue of debt has totally transformed higher education – at every level, I think. And the introduction of fees by Dearing in 1997, and their consolidation and extension by Brown in 2010, totally and almost instantaneously transformed the students' relationship not only to the universities, and to us as university employees, but to their futures. In some ways, I now think that one of the primary functions of the university, for the ruling class, is precisely to train a generation in indebtedness, in a state of being in debt. Higher education has become a kind of training ground for what is a long-term, lifelong experience of debt, and of acting as, functioning as, consumers. I feel very gloomy about that indeed.

YAQOOB   It is remarkable how rapidly universities were transformed in a small period, almost as if they were a microcosm of wider developments in the political economy of the United Kingdom. Debt-funding financial managers have been shoved into places that previously weren't managed on those terms. One of the struggles I think of which has been lost, or which was already lost, is the hope that seemingly fairly conservative universities and managers would resist marketisation and actually hold on to some sort of public good. Actually what we have seen from some vice-chancellors is that the upper-management cadres are now populated by people from finance. So there is not much chance of swinging the whole university sector around to oppose government policy. This is going to be like a civil war, for want of a better word.

BEAUMONT   Yeah, in the past it always seemed frankly precious or sententious to talk about the 'proletarianisation' of employees in higher education, and I can see that it risks still sounding like that to some people. But the younger generation of academics, people who are going into the profession now, are being proletarianised in some meaningful sense – they face more and more temporary contracts, less and less remunerative pay, inadequate pensions, and a foreclosing of their professional futures.

CAPILDEO   Of course it could be viewed as being feminised as well as proletarianised. Part-time or fixed-term ways of working are the non-choice choices into which women traditionally have been forced.

YAQOOB   And sectors that have a higher proportion of female participation tend to be regarded with less esteem and recognition. One of the things that was horrifying about teaching assessment exercises in the Teaching Excellence Framework was that it magnified some of the inequities in how people are recognised and understood as teachers and as providers of education. So in student assessments of teaching quality, women performed badly even when they were equal to men in all other forms of assessment. So what we're seeing is lots of the most pernicious aspects of British social development over the last twenty years being funnelled into the university as an institution.

VOCATION

CHARMAN   Is it time to think about this idea of academia as a vocation? The strike really brought to light precariousness, casualisation and how much the university relies upon the goodwill of its staff. This obviously puts those who have caring duties or aren't financially as well off or are single parents, for example, in a much worse position. Do you see academia as more than a job?

YAQOOB   I'm partly a political theorist, and maybe one of the most famous texts about politics as a vocation is Max Weber's lecture just after the First World War, and the language of that lecture is highly masculinised. It's about maintaining one's autonomy of judgement and being able to steer between an ethic of passionate conviction and an ethic of responsibility. It's also about being distinct from all the pressures of social reproduction. It's the idea that you might have a vocation that you are deeply invested in and that you value and that you can keep doing even if other pressures are knocking around. That to me seems almost unsustainable in this period: the idea that you can have a career path that fits this idea of vocation – lots of time for research, a sensible teaching workload – that you can fit around, say, caring responsibilities.

But on the other hand the idea of vocation also represents something quite dear to the ideas early career academics have of what a life in academia might be. An ability to manage your own time, to be free from direct management and pressure, to do something you really love. Unfortunately that now seems almost entirely ideological: the idea of putting extra time in because it is something you

are interested in, when you know your managers will squeeze as much out of you as possible.

CAPILDEO   I'm actually not in agreement with that description of vocation. Vocation literally, etymologically, means 'calling'. It is very interesting to me that the words 'vocation' and 'goodwill' were both used in the way the question was framed. I would resist and am in fact furious with such language, as that language belongs to religion and to churches. It suggests a value and reward in paradise or after death. But what that does is suggest that academics are mugs basically. [Laughter] That they can work themselves to death and have a certain amount of good feeling. It also means that because academics are mugs, if they feel good about their jobs they are also going to be mugged for their jobs. Whereas a lawyer or a financier who feels good about his job or her job is not expected to be mugged in the same way, and they're not told, 'Oh, do you have a vocation to be a barrister? Do you have a vocation to work for HMRC?' Nobody says that. I utterly resist that language. It's not goodwill labour if it's unpaid overtime by people who are suffering health consequences both physical and mental.

BEAUMONT   One independent consultancy company has estimated that academics in the UK do 40 million hours of unpaid labour, above and beyond the hours stipulated in their contract, each year and that this is worth more than £3 billion to the UK economy. So we are clearly exploited in that respect. I wouldn't entirely resist the notion of vocation though. I think I would want to cling to it in some ways and to defend the word in its secularised sense. Academics' responsibility, and passion, for provoking critical thinking in younger generations is an admirable one, albeit one that has to be conducted in increasingly embattled conditions. I would also argue that the business of research and writing can be vocational in a positive sense that is worth defending. David Harvey has a nice comment about his own academic writing and research, where he goes back to Marx's claim that Milton produced *Paradise Lost* simply because it was part of his species being, just as the silkworm produces silk. I'm not going to make any grandiloquent claims about my own species being, but I do want to go on researching and writing simply because it's what I do, it's what defines me. I just don't want to be exploited, restricted and trammelled in doing it.

CAPILDEO   I think this is an idealisation of

the academic, and also an underestimation of the dangers of white-washing and failing to decolonise the language one uses about education. It's impossible to adjust and reclaim a word and claim that it can be separate from its history, particularly when vocation isn't being applied across the board. You don't hear of a lot of people having a vocation to be an MP or a vocation to be a neurosurgeon, even though those require thorough and holistic dedication. That whole business of vocation and goodwill, that language that belongs to ritual and gets trotted in whenever people are underpaid. I see it happen in the arts as well.

YAQOOB   One thing that this raises is the fact that for certain sections of the university workforce the question has never really been about a vocation. If we think about STEM [Science, Technology, Engineering and Mathematics] subjects and working labs and commissions that are much more routinised and industry-funded, having this balance of teaching and research doesn't really make sense under those conditions. So, I suppose one question is – this is always in the back of my mind when we're organising in Cambridge – are we talking about the same kind of university? Are we talking about the same institution that's crisscrossed by different funding sources, from industry and large capital concerns? I agree there is some hard work to be done in thinking about the terminology we are using. I mean, we probably wouldn't say to someone on a zero hours contract that the way they should defend and improve their conditions is to think about it as a vocation. At the same time I can see why there are some elements of existential commitment to the profession that people want to hold on to. But I have to say that as an organiser that doesn't really help.

SACRIFICE

CHARMAN   I suppose we should think about the idea of sacrifice as well. Not to bring it back to religious language, but if you're working in such precarious conditions you have to then sacrifice elements of your personal life for that. To give you an example: I research maternity and economics in literature, and I am very aware of the irony that should I ever decide I want a child I don't think I could afford one, under the conditions of the sector as it is. I think people who are entering the profession now, people who are finishing their PhDs, are faced with having to choose between

aspects of their personal life and aspects of their professional life. So it's about sacrifice as well as vocation, maybe.

CAPILDEO   But that's two different things which are being brought together whenever that quasi-religious terminology is used. One is the conditions of work, and the other is the work that's being done and why. That is why I prefer terms like 'civil society', although they're flawed, because they imply at least some sort of future and collective vision rather than individual and inward movement.

YAQOOB   I think sacrifice is a telling word to be using there, because of course it could be used in the very individualised sense, but actually I think at the moment most early career academics would think of it as a much more ritualistic, bloody sacrifice. [Laughter] We're literally sacrificing our mental health, social life and relationships, on the altar of something that doesn't necessarily promise us that much in return. And there's a temporal aspect to this as well – what do we think these places are going to be like to work in in ten years? The sacrifice now doesn't necessarily mean better things ten years down the line, not after more pension cuts.

Vahni's comment about civil society is something I'd be interested in talking about more. The vision of society we are thinking of. I mean, we all like the idea of the university as some sort of engine of public good, but that's not really how we talk to students about the university. It's also not necessarily how our universities are set up to produce impact. On the one hand we have an impact agenda, and humanities people are familiar with that, but we also have state funding for certain purposes and we also have control of those funding streams. We get industry funding from places like British aerospace and other major industry sectors that need university expertise. But lots of these industries don't necessarily contribute to our vision of public good. What would a university dedicated to the pursuit of public good look like? That's something that's always bugged me. I don't have an idea of what that would be.

CAPILDEO   If there's an evisceration of the popular media through a lack of funding for expert journalists, burgeoning social media and the infiltration of the media sector by what I've heard called 'shadowy forces', and if we're not really able to move the government by being physical protesting bodies – if the place where people are supposed to be able to have a debate in education, or exercise critical thinking, or pursue an idea without an immediate outcome, if that place has to be transformed into something else – then what does a nation look like? What does a nation of voters look like in twenty-five years time? If I'm going to be idealistic, I would hope that the university would be a contributing force in the formation of the national psyche. But obviously that isn't how things are. Individual universities have different degrees of independence, different local pressures, and quite atomised reactions have been seen.

BEAUMONT   That's right. It still is a place where in some corners, more and more sequestered no doubt, critical thinking can be fostered. And a university system that is an unalloyed contribution to civil society and the public good would be one where, instead of being trained not to think, as effectively happens in all sorts of contexts in higher education at present, people were trained to think really critically. But the tools are there still and it's what many students still want. So however harried and harrassed, however compromised we are, I think that critical thinking is absolutely crucial to the positive vocation of the university sector.

UNDOING HIERARCHIES; INSTANT GRATIFICATION; FRUITFUL TEACHING

YAQOOB   I think there's something there. Maybe what we need to be talking about is ceding some of our hard-won pedagogical authority to students themselves. In my university that has meant a protest culture, a culture of decolonising subjects that academics had been thinking about decolonising but not in the sense of changing the structures of curriculums, for example. So I think this is something that has to be talked about and created with students, because it doesn't seem obvious to me that fees being increased has dimmed the critical protest culture we've had at our university. It's still there and it's still vibrant. It's under pressure in lots of ways, but that to me seems like the only way forward.

BEAUMONT   One of the great strengths of the expansion of the university in the late 1960s, and the protest movement with which it was interconnected, was a democratisation of relationships between students and staff. To some extent, this undid traditional pedagogic hierarchies, but we seem to have lost that. Of course, there are dangers in undoing those hierarchies as well, not least in further complicating an already very complex and delicate sort of sexual-political equilibrium. But I think that working towards a democratised relationship between staff and students is a very good thing, allowing students to set the agenda, to a greater extent.

CAPILDEO   I'm not sure whether it would be possible to do that without also having to be very careful. We are all old enough to remember what it was like not to have instant gratifying feedback. I remember having to write things by hand, memorise things and have three essays a week come back covered in red ink, without being able to get 101 likes for my picture of a cat or a flower. Isn't there a risk that anything that seems like hard work or pointless or niggling or unpleasant might be lost in a completely student-led learning space? One of the things in teaching I've found quite difficult is how to make the basic point that the criticism of an essay is not the criticism of a person, and that to suggest a particular way of formulating or expressing thought or pursuing research might require rethinking is not to question the fundamentals of the other person's being.

BEAUMONT   In a practical context, I teach in a department which still has a one-on-one tutorial system for each of its students throughout their three undergraduate years, and that close pedagogic relationship between staff member and student is superbly productive. Of course, it's completely unaffordable, and we're constantly under attack from the university management for clinging on to it in this conservative way that has become frankly radical in the current context. But it is the very best way of generating a stimulating intellectual environment, one where – precisely because, paradoxically, the relationship is personalised – the distinction between the work and the person can be disambiguated and can be rendered fruitful.

YAQOOB   I think that's quite a simple demand: if you want better degrees, pay for more teaching.

BEAUMONT   Precisely. Recruit large numbers of staff.

LIFELONG LEARNING; INTENDED HOSTILE ENVIRONMENTS

CHARMAN   Shouldn't we also be thinking about who gets to be a student in the first place? If we think of what's happening with the Open University right now – it's arguably been the hardest hit by the increase of tuition fees, which has lowered its student numbers by a third, as well as ideological funding cuts – and the increasing difficulties for part-time and mature students, they're things to consider when we talk about things like access and social good. The crisis in further education is limiting who actually gets to go to university in the first place.

YAQOOB   The Open University has its headquarters in our trade union region so we organise together with trade union organisers from Further Education colleges and the Open University. The cuts delivered year on year into further education are just astonishing. Considering the job losses, how some of these institutions keep their core functions going is extraordinary. One of the dangers of being on the front line in higher education institutions is that university starts being talked about like it's a one-shot thing: you've got to get them at 16, get them in for three years and if they mess up they're screwed and have wasted a lot of money. There has to be a stronger sense that these are institutions for lifelong learning. There should be ways for people to come back in, to drop out, to not feel like they've failed because three years didn't go well. I think lots of universities would say that's not their job, that they should just be talking about access, about getting people through that gate at the beginning of the three-year degree. Actually if there's one virtue of having a national solidaristic sector like this one, it's that it has a way of bringing a collective voice to bear on government.

CAPILDEO   I absolutely agree about the need for education to be lifelong. If education has to begin at university level, in effect what that means is that universities are being asked to make up suddenly and in one shot for all the inequalities that a person has experienced from birth. As though suddenly and miraculously after one gateway exam the university can begin to address inequalities in how a person's carers have been able to provide for them, their nutrition, their upbringing and their schooling. That's an insane responsibility and it's setting the university up to fail. And I do really feel universities are being set up to fail.

This isn't a huge jump: there have been some critiques of what's been happening recently with the persecution and deportation of the Windrush generation which say that it's not a failure of government, that these are the intended effects of a hostile environment. I would agree with that.

I think there's an intended hostile environment against in-depth critical thinking and one-to-one communication. If you have one-to-one communication you equip individuals to resist mass messages. If you want to govern a mass population by a populist rhetoric then you are not going to invest in an institution which furthers individual critical thinking. So considering this environment, how can you still use a phrase like 'the university has a voice to bear on the government'? What does that even mean?

YAQOOB   I suppose – this sounds increasingly insane as I prepare my thinking here – if UUK [Universities UK] as the collective voice of universities were able to say to the Department of Education that certain reforms miss the fact that universities can't pick up the pieces and could make the case for funding our sister institutions in further education better, then that could be useful.

CAPILDEO   Why would the government be interested in this?

YAQOOB   Well, I don't think they would be.

CAPILDEO   That's really what I'm asking. The university is also a place where you can indoctrinate people, or replicate ideologies. It's not just a neutral space. There's a craft in education just like there's a craft in poetry. People often go on as if poets should be intrinsically more virtuous people, because poetry is inspiring and uplifting, but historically poets were the paid propagandists of whoever was rich or happened to have won the latest war. The epics that we know and find so much nuance in are patronised propaganda for a large part.

YAQOOB   Depends who wins the next war.

CAPILDEO   That's the thing, isn't it. A war mentality. Universities need to be much more hawkish.

BEAUMONT   There is something self-destructive about the government's, and about capital's, failure to invest in higher education, because by their own criteria there is an enormous benefit, economically, to having a widely and highly educated workforce. Okay, of course the capitalist system needs people who aren't going to think critically; it wants people who aren't aspirational. But, given the nature of post-industrial capitalism, it increasingly needs a technologically trained, educated workforce. In spite of this, the government and capital don't seem to be particularly interested in that. That debate isn't happening.

YAQOOB   I suppose the problem is that it's

not just capital, or this particular government, it's Britain. It's a particular model of productivity that British capitalism has. It's about underinvestment, it's about squeezing as much profit out with as little investment in infrastructure and training as you can get away with. Obviously this Conservative government is just carrying on from previous governments. It can't be left to whatever government picks up the pieces in five or ten years to come up with a brand new policy to reform the sector. Some of this thinking has to come from within the institutions themselves, and it can't be left to our vice-chancellors. So I suppose when I say a collective voice I don't mean UUK. I mean something like a totally renovated trade union with a new leadership.

THE CULTURE OF SILENCE

CHARMAN   I wondered if we could talk explicitly about diversity and equality as policy within universities. Sara Ahmed in her work on diversity in institutions, which I'm sure you're all familiar with, talks about the gap between symbolic commitments to diversity and equality and the experience of those who embody them, and how diversity policies are used as evidence that universities don't have a problem with racism or don't have a problem with sexism, or sexual harassment. What would a meaningful diversity policy look like in a university?

YAQOOB   I can be very wonkish and boring about this. Cambridge has 'Breaking the Silence', which is a fairly new initiative. It's genuinely valuable. It's an opportunity for people to report things anonymously and have them taken seriously. But once things are in, academic staff will then be put through the standard old disciplinary procedures, with the same standards of proof required that means lots of cases are thrown out immediately. 'Breaking the Silence' had the involvement of staff and union members, and Cambridge Rape Crisis were also on board. It shows that universities can go a few extra steps and arrive at something that genuinely gathers information and takes people seriously, and yet it might risk having nothing but a symbolic effect. Nothing will change unless there's a serious change to disciplinary policies that actually threatens university staff's employment. Otherwise you have a situation where people simply go on gardening leave and come back after a year or two.

BEAUMONT   Thinking about sexual harassment specifically, even when these new procedures are put in place they don't necessarily have a really concrete and productive effect... The long-term consequences might well be suspension on full pay, for individuals who are guilty of scandalous behaviour towards young people who they're exploiting in power terms as well as sexually. Indeed, these individuals often end up getting more embedded in institutions because in effect, and for good reason, they're disqualified from going out on the open market and looking for jobs elsewhere. They get more and more rooted in departments, the reputations of which get more and more damaged. So I think the reforms really have to be ruthless. The regulations have to be clearly written into contracts from the very beginning, and there has to be total transparency and accountability.

CAPILDEO   I'd quite like to get back beyond what policies *are*, because this is reminding me a little bit of what Dr Claire Marris from the City University of London was saying in one of the USS [Universities Superannuation Scheme] briefs. She talked about how the pension system treats the experience of white heterosexual men as the default. And that can be the case, I think, around harassment, even with the most well-read diversity or inclusivity policies. Because, for example, we need to ask, what is good testimony? And for that the university needs to do more joined-up thinking, in that within a university there will be psychologists, lawyers, and scientists who have cutting-edge research on trauma and the effect of memory. So before you even ask people to make statements, or act as witnesses, ask, what does it mean to have a memory? What is a statement? That's not a sort of purely theoretical question.

YAQOOB   People who suffer sexual harassment or abuse of power are taken, even in worthwhile initiatives like 'Breaking the Silence', to be whistleblowers, right? It's like there's a secure Dropbox you can drop your complaint into. They're never treated as actors with their own context and history. Which means the broader culture that enables these kinds of things isn't really tackled. A department will engage with one person who's responsible. So there has to be something other than this individualistic model of whistleblowing. And the other thing I've noticed from doing union casework is that people don't go forward with complaints on their own. They need support to be able to do that. In fact, even the other staff members who support students making these complaints come under pressure from within their department, so they need support too.

CAPILDEO   If a sexual harassment complaint is cast as individual and legalistic it's a misunderstanding of the nature of that complaint. And therefore the policy is inadequate. Because a policy of report suggests you can say 'I have been harassed' in the same way that you'd say 'My handbag was stolen and I lost £20, a lipstick, a passport and two books.' Whereas sometimes to make a sexual harassment complaint isn't to report an offence but to begin a process of discovering what happened. Sometimes it's in the process of reporting and being supported or unsupported that a person sorts out what actually happened there.

SPREADSHEETS;
PRIVILEGE; NAMES

CHARMAN   I don't know if any of you have seen the spreadsheet that's currently circulating?
CAPILDEO   That's so interesting, can I ask you a question?
CHARMAN   Yes.
CAPILDEO   I recently had this conversation with people from different backgrounds: north, south, genuinely working-class, genuinely privileged, white, non-white, but all in bodies presenting as female. Though we're not all female-identified. But basically we walk through the world being treated as female. And I only knew about the spreadsheet from looking on Twitter. One of my friends had seen the spreadsheet but not the way to access it. Another one had been told about what was happening but had not seen the spreadsheet and didn't know how to access it. So that again expresses part of the problem: that there's a kind of whisper culture. What do you think is your intersection of privilege such that you have all this knowledge? And can you tell us about the spreadsheet?
CHARMAN   So the spreadsheet is 'Time's Up Academia'. It's a version of the Shitty Media Men spreadsheet that caused a huge furore earlier this year. And it's just an Excel editable spreadsheet. It's anonymous in that that you'll fill in which institution, where it happened, what you were at the time, who the perpetrator was, and then a description of the incident, and how long ago it was. And the intersection of my privilege that allowed me to access it is probably just that I saw

it on Twitter. So I guess it's that thing of following the right people and having an online community, a whisper network that is just made manifest.
CAPILDEO   I have major disagreements and minor disagreements with the spreadsheet, even though I agree that the lid should be blown off what's going on. If there's a spreadsheet circulating with descriptions of incidents and locations but no names, what is being invited there or encouraged is for us to play a kind of cryptic puzzle game. Because many people are brought up on games as children. And in the UK we're brought up in a test culture. There are rewards for getting the answer. But what is the mentality then? The mentality is one where we start undertaking surveillance on our neighbours. If people feel that it's OK to start playing guessing games about who might have done what, it only takes a tiny little turn to start checking up on other things. It's a checking-up mentality... Which is interesting.
YAQOOB   My sense is that a spreadsheet like this would not have been possible if it was broken down per institution. Precisely because people would be so unwilling to report anonymously knowing that the perpetrator would be able to guess it was them complaining. Which again speaks to the inequity or the total absence of any meaningful structures that would side with the people who are the targets.
CAPILDEO   This is why I worry that not naming the perpetrators on the document is actually a retrogressive move and that a straight down the line witch hunt would be a progressive move. Because otherwise it's just kind of shifting the burden.
CHARMAN   Is a way of thinking about the spreadsheet then not as data but as a resource of testimony? That it might provide solidarity? Unless these things are documented people won't realise that their experience was common, or that their experience was harassment or was something that they have a right to feel how they do about. Because it's an enormous, enormous spreadsheet. Just scrolling through it people can say, 'That's happened to me, that's happened to me.'
CAPILDEO   Or perhaps find reflected there their own experience for which they didn't have words.
YAQOOB   And realise things that happened to them were things rather than just the everyday they have to put up with.
CAPILDEO   That's very important, yeah.

YAQOOB   So where does it go from here? Between having this data to actually being able to do something like what Me Too did? Well it probably does require names, actually.

CAPILDEO   Yeah, I think it actually does. Otherwise there's an embodiment of survivors/victims but there's a faceless monster perpetrator. Because there will be a particularity to every story that's given, but there's no particularity to the perpetrator.

YAQOOB   And students leave, is the other thing. They leave after a few years and it's very hard, the idea of going back and pursuing something like that, when in some cases they would rather not be constantly questioned and asked to give proof and data. It's very easy for these institutions, more than ordinary workplaces, to just sit these things out. So we have to rely on the collective memory. Things might have to be taken up as causes not by the people who make the complaints themselves. I think that's really problematic as well. Does a student who leaves want an afterlife to their complaint that they're not in control of?

CAPILDEO   Which in itself suggests that at a policy level there needs to be a fundamental rethinking of what a policy is. Presumably there must be some way for a person not to lose agency without requiring them to be crucified as a present witness.

YAQOOB   Representation at a conceptual level. Someone who is mandated to represent. It doesn't have to be an individual, it could be a body of complaint. But you have to have a structure that allows that to be possible.

CAPILDEO   Shouldn't there be a sort of policy at some point to detach? Where it's possible to detach and say, 'I have given this testimony which will now be handed over for use', like giving a blood sample or something. 'It's no longer part of me, it's yours to do your thing with.'

CHARMAN and YAQOOB   Yeah.

'YOU CARRY YOUR POWER STRUCTURE WITH YOU.'

CAPILDEO   Actually, that makes me think of something I hadn't been able to articulate before. Which had been worrying me about democratisation. I'm not sure that people who are in a position of authority always know that they have a representative role. Because they go on thinking of themselves as individuals. Like that cliché of how someone who's 90-something, still feels 25 inside. But I think there's also a way in which people's self-image doesn't catch up. So when there are students appearing to be powerful or equal or articulate and there are academics who are unaware that they themselves are incarnate institutional power, those academics need to have their consciousness seriously raised. Because I don't think these academics know that if they're in a room with one of these supposedly 'powerful' students, they're not an individual in a room with another individual. They're an entire college or a degree result in the room.

CHARMAN   I heard a senior academic in my institution speak about how the problem of sexual harassment in universities was that certain behaviour had been brought into the world of the university. The implication being that if a student and a professor had sex off campus that would be fine. Because you don't carry your power structure with you.

CAPILDEO   But you do.

CHARMAN   Well exactly.

BEAUMONT   But, on the other hand, I've known students who I regard as having been seriously abused because they've had relationships with people teaching them – and this partly goes back to your point about how we have a virtual sense of ourselves – and nonetheless believed they were co-responsible for what happened. So I think both academics and students have a mistaken conception of this. And it's partly about educating both parties effectively.

CAPILDEO   I mean quite simply that when one's in a continuing or responsible role one ceases to be a personal person.

BEAUMONT   Absolutely. You're the bearer of values.

CAPILDEO   I was thinking about this recently, how ten years ago I wouldn't have thought anything of working on a presentation in my room with a couple of colleagues. But now I no longer wish to do that. Because I don't want to set a precedent or an example.

'ACADEMICS WHO LIVE SACRIFICIALLY ARE SETTING TERRIBLE EXAMPLES.'

YAQOOB   This is going off on a bit of a tangent, but it is about representation. It's about action-short-of-strike and working to contract.

Something happened where people suddenly felt that their working habits, how they arranged their day, became politicised. If you were emailing people outside of your hours you were breaking rank, you were reinforcing the model of the university. And I thought that was a really remarkable moment where people simply stopped thinking of their private working lives as private but actually understood that they were simply reproducing structures. And for students who were getting emails at 11 p.m. or whatever, academics were passing on a really nefarious knowledge about what working life is supposed to be like.

CAPILDEO   I was thinking this earlier when we were talking about sacrifice and vocation. And I was thinking that academics who live sacrificially are setting terrible examples. Even if students don't go into academia, what am I telling that student? I'm telling that student that midnight is a working hour.

YAQOOB   I mean, it really does tilt against the ideology of a vocation. Because it's precisely the ideology of a vocation that would encourage someone to send that email.

CAPILDEO   Yes, unless you actually returned to the proper monastic vocation, in which case you would have hours to do things, and at that hour you'd be engaged in something else. So the academic 'vocation' is kind of like vocation run mad, or vocation drunk at the steering wheel. [Laughter] Also, a basic question which I found wasn't addressed was why working to contract should be punishable. Why does a contract exist with the intention that it would be violated? Why are people working to void contracts most of the time?

YAQOOB   Yes, it really says something, that that sacrificial model is enshrined in your contract. Most people are not given any defined working hours at all. You're left with an open future, it's up to your department to decide what's a reasonable amount of working time to complete your duties, and your duties are open-ended.

CAPILDEO   That's why I found it very interesting to work in culture for development. There was an understanding that, for example, if a writer was giving a workshop, we wouldn't just say, that's three hours of face-to-face workshop leading. We'd say, that's half a day or one-and-a-half days' preparation plus half a day's travel. There was a question of accounting for the intangible labour.

YAQOOB   And a means to reproduce life rather than simply remuneration for the value that's generated for the institution. I think one of the things universities evidently don't care about is understanding an employee as an individual with their own arc through life, with other plans, other than producing things for certain boxes like the REF. We need a radical decommodification of the academic workforce. You're right, the vocation thing is a terrible term to invoke right now because we're at a cusp where we can understand ourselves as workers with rights and entitlements and value.

CHARMAN   It's strange how despite zero hours contracts being set up as a concrete thing where if you teach for one hour you'll get paid for one hour, you're then often not paid on time. You are conceived of as a purely economic unit, yet the fact that you will then be paying bills every month, and paying your rent – which the university charges you, and which is very high – is not taken into consideration when payment comes around, because it's still taken to be this kind of nebulous, non-market system.

CAPILDEO   This is where I would agree that the system's intended to fail. It's a way of ensuring that the ones who are fittest to survive will be the ones chasing funding…

YAQOOB   Or relying on dwindling reserves of family wealth. There's an inequity aspect about entering academia. Who gets to enter the university and who gets to enter academic life? Well, it's people who have the stock and the reserves to sustain those hungry months and years.

CHARMAN   Catherine Oakley has spoken on Twitter about the fact that if you're on a PhD stipend you're living under the poverty line, according to the Institute of Fiscal Studies.

CAPILDEO   It's quite interesting because of the knock-on effect for anti-diversity and anti-inclusivity, because people who can't afford to be at university will not be able to bring the perspectives about what is actually needed to change the university, to make it inclusive of them.

CHARMAN   It's a narrowing of perspective that's harmful to the university itself.

CAPILDEO   It harms the university if it's the ideal university. It's fine if it becomes the replicant body for our ruling class.

YAQOOB   It's very helpful then, actually.

See p. 188 for a list of further reading.

GREEN_FIELDS
MARIA HUMMER

FICTION

We were told to pay attention to things that were different, and it seemed to me that sex was no longer the same. Now, we always wondered if someone was watching. It wasn't clear to us which sections were private, and how the technology worked. It was also hard not to picture our real bodies somewhere in the frozen dark, motionless while we moved together here in the seeming warm.

I brought it up in my sessions with the Reverend. He told me he was surprised it had taken me so long to ask. The others had worried about it in Cycle 1.

'Which Cycle are we in?' I asked. It was difficult to keep track.

'Cycle 3,' said the Reverend. 'I understand your concern, but of course nobody watches you. It was part of the privacy agreement we signed at the start. Don't you remember?'

I did. That is, I hadn't until the Reverend mentioned it. The memory was there, but it felt very far away. And maybe it was. We hadn't been told precisely how long the experiment would take. We wouldn't know until we were unfrozen at the end, our bodies still in their thirties and our minds at god-knows-what age.

But the money was good. Sam and I would be able to afford a nice wedding and a honeymoon to Hawaii, and only one of us would need to work while the other stayed home with the kids we hoped to have. That is, if we were still fertile at the end. It was one of the risks.

Our life together before the VR world was still clear in my mind and I looked back on it often: Sam and me walking together to rehearsals, our first kiss in the snow, our apartment above Shipley Automotive, taking care of each other through winter fevers. Our memories made in the VR world were less acute, but we were happy, we had each other, and we never got sick.

Only couples were accepted for the experiment – 'deeply committed couples', in fact, and there was a test we had had to take to determine how committed we were. One of the questions was: 'If you were offered a place in heaven without your partner, would you still go?' We both selected 'no'. The other people in the experiment were Manny and Blake, childhood sweethearts who wanted the money to raise a family, and Susan and Letitia, who planned to start a business together when they got out. 'I just hope no one else thinks of our idea in the meantime,' said Letitia. The six of us were sitting around the table in the communal space, experiencing – it was difficult to think of it as 'eating' – dinner. That day it was paella, wafting cartoonish puffs of steam. There was obviously no need to eat, but the routine kept us sane. It was for this same reason that we retired to our own rooms after dinner to watch TV with our partners and sleep.

'What's your idea?' asked Manny.

'I'm not telling you,' said Letitia. 'You'll steal it if you get out first.'

'If I remember it,' said Manny.

There was an order of departure from the experiment that none of us understood. We had all begun at the same time, but so far we'd already said goodbye to two couples, including a pair who had had to leave several days apart from each other. I tried to ask the Reverend about it in our sessions, but he wouldn't explain.

'We're contractually obliged to tell you everything when you wake up,' he said, 'but not before.'

The Reverend was the only one who came and went between worlds. We knew he had assistants, but none of them ever joined us here. If the Reverend needed help with something in the VRW, he'd use one of us. It's what we were there for.

We all had our tasks. We weren't allowed to discuss them with anyone but our partners, so I wasn't sure what everybody else did all day. I wasn't even really sure what Sam did, because his task was to assist the Reverend, so it required an additional level of secrecy. I was adept at spatial reasoning, according to a massive test I'd taken before the start of the experiment, so my tasks usually involved exploring buildings or landscapes. I wandered through forests, fields, gardens, palaces, and rooms whose doors never led to the same place twice. I was often given the same bright green hillside with purple blossoms and blue sky. Sometimes I'd hike for what seemed like hours and never reach the top. Other times I'd take just a few steps and suddenly be heading down the other side.

There was a stream in the hillside landscape. Sometimes it was at the bottom of the hill, sometimes not. I walked around, picked flowers, skipped stones. Often the flowers would disappear moments after being picked; other times they refused to be picked at all. Once the grass wouldn't give at my footsteps and I had to walk gingerly along the tips. These were glitches and I was supposed to record them out loud. 'Glitch: grass doesn't bend when I step on it.' 'Glitch: stream floating one foot off the ground.' 'Glitch: tree swaying like a loose rope.' Once in a while the glitch was so astonishing – like one time when the landscape just ended and I found myself walking and not walking through a weird grey nothing – that I would forget to record it, I would just look around with my mouth open.

After each of these sessions I filled out a short form. The form would ask me to report, for example, if I had seen a bird, what it had been perching on, and what colour it had been. Often I couldn't remember. We had all signed an honesty agreement before entering the experiment and I didn't want to forfeit my payment by getting caught in a lie, so I would write, 'I don't remember.' Many of my completed forms were filled with I-don't-remembers.

Every week – every month? year? it was difficult to tell – we would have a Group Challenge. On these days we would gather in the Reverend's workshop, where he gave each of us an envelope with our instructions inside. *Find the cat. Search for and report any instances of the colour blue.* Sometimes we'd all have the same task, but other times they would be conflicting, like when Letitia and I were told to make sure nobody went in the caves, and everyone else had to try to get into them. Teamwork, problem solving, conflict resolution. The Group Challenges often took place in landscapes I had explored, and some of the challenges seemed to be timed, because back in his Workshop the Reverend would comment on occasion, 'In record speed.'

We begged to be told how long in Outside Hours – OH for short – these challenges took, but the only thing the Reverend ever told us in real OH was that our nights were three hours long. 'Enough to dream,' he said. But I never did.

Some people had difficulty adjusting to the VRW in the beginning. Letitia begged for the chance to video-call her sister, but we weren't allowed to contact anyone in the RW. It was all there in the contracts we signed. Letitia grew depressed. She began to eat whenever, whatever she could. There were no consequences like gaining weight, but the Reverend still called her in for extra sessions. VRW or not, sadness is still sadness. An addiction still an addiction.

Sam and I were relatively fine. Our families respected our decision and we had no regrets. The tough part for me, though, was getting used to walking without feeling myself walk. In the VRW if you wanted to move in a particular direction you thought about it and it happened, but you didn't feel your knees bend and creak like you did in the RW. I was a dancer. I was used to the sensation of my own body in space. I mentioned this to the Reverend.

'And does that get in the way of your enjoyment of life here?' he asked.

I thought about it. Really, it was more than just the walking and moving. It was the sex. Our bodies didn't feel like bodies in each other's hands. I missed our clumsy knees, our animal stench.

'I would say it does,' I replied.

But that was in the beginning. Either the Reverend followed up on my comments and tweaked the programming, or I just got used to it.

'Do you think the Reverend is real?' I asked Sam one evening in our room. The window was open to some simulation of a warm breeze. The brilliantly constellated night sky was like a mix between a Van Gogh painting and the kind of stars you remember from childhood.

'He's not physically real, no,' said Sam. 'But neither are we.'

'But is he a representation of a real person, like us?' I asked. 'Susan thinks maybe they're testing artificial intelligence. They want to see how long we all take orders from a thing without realising.'

'How do you know Susan is real?' said Sam.

'Because we met her,' I said. 'In the orientation, in the RW, remember? The day before they – before the start of this whole thing.'

It was still difficult to say *before they froze us*.

In the RW Sam was a musician. He had been in the orchestra for one of my dance shows, and that was how we'd met. In our VRW apartment he'd been given a piano, a sleek baby grand, something we could never afford outside. But when Sam sat down to play, the music sounded awful. It sounded like a piano, but it was too perfect, too much in tune. He asked the Reverend if it could be fixed, but the Reverend had trouble understanding exactly what the problem was. He said he would look into it, and the piano stayed the same.

The music was supposed to be confined to our apartment, but at times a glitch meant that I could hear it in a different section of the world. Sound was something the programmers seemed to have real trouble with. In the RW, sound waves are born and die in a fixed location as dictated by the laws of science. But in the VRW the laws had to be carefully programmed, which meant details were often overlooked. Sometimes I would hear Letitia and Susan talking even though they were nowhere in sight. Other times I would be startled by someone suddenly appearing behind me because the programme didn't generate the sound of their footsteps.

Occasionally bigger glitches happened. Like I'd roll over in bed and fall straight through the floor, landing in some half-finished chamber with walls that started and ended nowhere. Sometimes I would get stuck in a terrifying loop, first in one place and then suddenly in another, or I'd see Sam in two places at once, or I'd hear his voice behind my shoulder saying something he'd tried to say an hour ago, or even further in the past. One time I saw a duck near a pond in one of my landscapes, nuzzling its head under its wing. As I stepped closer it turned and looked at me and I swear it had the face of my grandmother.

The system crashed once, very early into the experiment, and we all blacked out for a while, hearing nothing, seeing nothing, only aware of the passing of time. When the world flickered back, I found myself climbing a spiral staircase in a tower. Manny was waiting at the top. One by one the others arrived too. Sam was the last, followed soon after by the Reverend. Then we all turned around silently and went back downstairs, ending up in the familiar common room. Susan thought maybe we had all woken for a moment in our boxes. The Reverend would neither confirm nor deny this.

The system almost crashed again in Cycle 2 when Letitia, leading a 'revolt', tried to force an overload by bombarding the programme with requests. She recruited everyone to her cause – even me, even Sam. Nothing much happened, just a few warning pop-ups sprouting at our feet and sailing into the sky, bearing cryptic codes like P2overDS1. The Reverend stopped us before it could get too far.

'I appreciate this is difficult for you,' he said, 'but please bear in mind the agreement you signed. Any action taken in opposition to the spirit of the study puts you at risk of forfeiting your end payment.'

'Tell us what you're testing,' said Letitia. 'Tell us how long it's been.'

'We will,' said the Reverend.

Then he told us he had a surprise. A brand new programme had just been finished, a flight programme, which every single one of us had been requesting since the start. We spent a happy day – a happy week? – soaring around a sunny hillside, whooping and laughing, and the revolt was forgotten. Flying – it felt so familiar. Like all the dreams I wished I'd had.

*

We entered Cycle 4. I couldn't remember how many cycles there were supposed to be in total. I wanted to ask the Reverend in my sessions, but it was beginning to be embarrassing how little my memory retained. It seemed like every session I asked him a question I'd already asked, possibly several times before. Often these questions were about Sam.

'We might be having trouble in our relationship,' I said.

'I know,' said the Reverend. 'We discussed this last time.'

'Oh. And what was your answer last time?'

He said something but I wasn't listening. In fact, I'd already forgotten my question.

'Is there anything else?' he asked.

'No,' I said. 'Yes. Why do we call you the Reverend?'

The Reverend laughed. 'This question again,' he said.

I felt annoyed. It wasn't my fault I asked the same questions again and again. Weren't the programmers supposed to be working on memory retention?

'You know,' he said, 'you're actually the only one who calls me that.'

'I am?'

'My name is Alexander.'

'Why do I call you the Reverend?'

'I don't know,' he said.

*

It was time for a Group Challenge. We met in the Reverend's Workshop for our envelopes. I opened mine. It was blank.

'Excuse me,' I said.

'No time for questions,' said the Reverend.

He opened a door to a small room and told us to wait inside. The door closed. We all looked at each other with tight smiles. Things were always a little tense at the beginning of a Group Challenge.

I wanted Sam to put his arm around me but I knew he wouldn't. Lately he'd begun to seem very far away. He didn't talk to me as much as he used to, but he couldn't share what he was working on with the Reverend so there wasn't a lot we could talk about. We used to pass the time reminiscing about life before the experiment, or planning our wedding for afterwards, but lately when I mentioned these things he got strange and quiet. I wished our real bodies weren't in separate boxes, in different rooms, because at least physical closeness makes emotional distance easier to bear. The first thing I wanted to do when the experiment was over was hold Sam, really hold him, smell his neck, smell his hair.

The door opened again. It led to what seemed to be a train station platform.

We walked onto it. There were three benches. Manny and Blake took one, Susan and Letitia took another. I sat down on the third and expected Sam to join me but he didn't. He paced around, and then stood in front of a map and tried to read it, squinting his eyes. A habit. Squinting wouldn't make things any easier to read here. I joined him and we looked at the map together. It was all slanted and skewed, like we were looking at it through moving water.

'Guys,' said Blake, 'this is our train.'

A train was pulling into the station. No one was driving it and there were no other passengers in its six cars.

'How do you know?' said Letitia. 'Was that written in your envelope?'

'I just know we have to get on.'

The train doors slid open and we entered. We saw that the seats were labelled. Blake and Manny sat beneath their names. Susan and Letitia saw their names further down the car. I followed them. They sat down and I kept walking. In the next car I found my name above a seat, but it was all by itself. I didn't see Sam's name anywhere. That's when I realised he wasn't following me. I was all alone.

I looked around. There he was, on the platform. The doors were already shut.

'Wait,' I said. 'We need to wait for Sam.'

I ran to a window and called to him to get on. He just smiled and shrugged, lifting the piece of paper from his envelope: *Don't board the train.*

I didn't like what was happening. We had never done a Group Challenge without Sam. I tried to open the train door but it wouldn't budge. 'Open,' I said. And then, 'Glitch. Door won't open. Please open door.'

The train started to move.

'Wait,' I shouted. Sam got further away and then he was gone. The train sped up, heading for a tunnel. The tunnel was dark. Everything dissolved. I could hear the train running on the tracks but I could no longer see or feel anything.

And then I was struck with a sensation so intense I knew instantly, horribly, that it was *real*.

My body tingled. My fingertips, my toes. Everything tingled like I had been plugged into an electrical socket and was being turned on. The roar of the train grew louder.

'Sam,' I tried to yell, but no sound was made.

*

Voices first, and then the light. People talking. Shadows as hands passed silver instruments above my head. The light. I felt it in my entire body like a cramp. 'She's back,' someone said, and the room quieted down and emptied until it was just me and a woman in a white coat.

'Sam,' I croaked.

'Shh,' said the woman. 'Relax. Take your time.'

I blinked. Or maybe I fell asleep, because when I opened my eyes the woman was in a different part of the room. I asked for Sam again. It was difficult to find the energy. Everything felt slow and heavy – my body, the air around me.

'Try to relax,' she said.

I turned my head and saw a window. The world outside was dull, grey, lost in a cloud. It was all wrong.

The woman said something but I didn't catch it.

'What?' I said.

'What?' she said.

'You said something.'

'You mean when I asked if you wanted anything to eat? That was almost half an hour ago.'

'No, you said...' I could barely get the words out. I choked, then started to retch. The woman hurried over with a bucket and caught my vomit. She wiped my face.

When I opened my eyes again there was a different person in the room, fiddling with some things inside a drawer.

'Where's the Reverend?' I asked. My voice didn't sound like my own.

The person looked up. 'Who?'

'The Reverend.'

The person didn't answer. He just wrote something on a clipboard and walked away.

I slept again.

When I woke, someone was coming into the room. The woman in the white coat. She sat beside my bed and crossed her legs.

'How are you feeling?' she asked.

Feeling. How was I feeling? I didn't know. There was too much. The heat of my legs under blankets. The whirring of machines in my room and down the hall. The beat of my heart, which felt too fast. An ache in my elbows and knees. A thirst so powerful I felt it everywhere.

'Water,' I said.

She smiled and brought me a cup. I needed help sitting up, and then when I tried to drink the water I coughed most of it back up. She patted my back gently until the coughing was done. I tried again, and managed to drink most of it.

'There you go,' she said. She wrote something down on a clipboard. 'Are you having trouble with the passage of time?'

'What?'

'What?' she said. Her legs were crossed the other way now. When had she shifted?

The clipboard in her hands was gone.

'Glitch,' I said.

'There are no glitches here,' she said.

'But I saw...'

'Just rest,' she said, standing up. 'We'll talk more later.'

I didn't want her to go. I needed some questions answered, but I couldn't remember what they were.

'Wait,' I said.

She turned and waited patiently.

'Where...'

I needed to know where something was. No, someone. Someone important. I could feel it right in the centre of my chest. My heart. Sam.

'Where's Sam?' I asked.

'Later,' was all she said. She left the room.

The night was impossibly long. I knew it was night because the grey outside the window had turned black. There were no stars.

I slept a little, and I woke to black. I slept a little more, and woke to still more black. How long could one night be?

I was suspicious of everything around me. I didn't know if it was truly the real world, or if it was a Group Challenge gone horribly wrong. I was too weak to get out of my bed, so I waited.

After a fourth waking, the light outside had finally changed. People moved around outside my room. Finally, the woman in the white coat entered and said my name.

'There's someone here who'd like to see you,' she said.

I tried to sit up. My heart fluttered, expecting Sam. But instead a grey-haired woman walked in. She had a cane. Her face was familiar in a way I didn't like. She said something to me.

'What?' I said. It was hard to make out because she was crying.

She covered her mouth with her hand and said something else. It sounded like maybe she was saying my name.

'Grandma?' I asked.

She shook her head no. The woman in the white coat led her out.

When she came back, the woman in the white coat said, 'Alright. I'm ready now.'

I was confused. 'For what?' I asked.

'Didn't you have some questions you wanted to ask me?'

Did I? I wasn't sure.

'Who are you?' I asked.

'We went over this yesterday,' she said.

'I thought the programmers were going to fix the memory problem,' I said. 'The Reverend told me.'

'The memory problem is fixed. But you're in the real world now.'

I looked around. Things were dull and grey, yes, but they were too sharp, too clear to be anything but virtual.

The woman was speaking to me. I knew I should focus on her words but it was difficult.

'I need to see the Reverend,' I said. 'Is the Group Challenge over yet?'

'Yes,' said the woman. She frowned. 'It's all over. The experiment is done.'

'The Reverend always talks to us when the Group Challenge is over.'

'You're talking to him now. As I have explained.'

I felt sick. I had a stomach ache, and then it moved to my head. I had a queasy head.

'It's all over?'

'Yes.'

'That can't be right.' I was remembering something. Something from long before. 'Sam and I were supposed to wake up in the same room. You... they told us. We were going to wake up together.'

There was a tap on the door and someone else came in. Another person in a white coat. 'How's it going?' he asked the woman softly, as if I was sleeping and he didn't want to wake me.

'Her memory retention,' she started to explain, also in a whisper, but I missed the rest of her words.

They whispered together for a while. Most of it was nonsense but I caught the phrase, 'four other test subjects'.

'Five other test subjects,' I mumbled.

They looked at me.

'There are six of us. Me and Sam and... Where's Sam?'

My words were garbled, and my attention was too; I wasn't sure my question was fully understood, and I struggled to focus as the woman in the white coat answered it.

'What?' I said.

She pointed at a stack of yellowed papers on the bedside table. I picked them up. The edges of the papers were curling and they were held together with a rusty staple. It was the agreement that Sam and I had signed before entering the VRW. I flipped through it and saw that some words were underlined in fresh ink: 'strictly confidential', 'waives the right to discuss, share, or otherwise acknowledge', and then, towards the end, 'death'. This last word was underlined twice. I read its sentence carefully.

'Both parties acknowledge that they are embarking upon the assignment as a deeply committed couple and, further, in the event of one party's failure to complete the assignment, be it for reason of illness, death, or otherwise, the other party agrees to complete the assignment in full...'

I couldn't read any further. My eyes skipped to the bottom of the page, where Sam's and my signatures had been scrawled. The ink was faded.

Something strange was happening to my eyes. They were leaking, making my cheeks wet. Alarmed, I was about to ask if this was another horrible side effect. And then I remembered tears.

'What were you testing?' I asked, but there was no one there to answer my question. I was alone.

I found that another piece of paper had appeared on my lap. A pamphlet. On the cover was a picture of a familiar hillside. Words on the top said: Welcome to *Green Fields*... And then on the bottom: *...forever!*

I let the pamphlet fall to the floor.

I stayed still for a while, just lying there. More tears were coming but they stopped eventually. Then it occurred to me that I'd already done so much lying down inside the frozen box that I didn't want to do it any more. I thought about sitting up. I was confused when my body didn't move, but then I remembered I would have to do it myself. That's how things worked here. I pressed my palms to the bed, tensed my muscles, and pushed myself up. For the first time in a lifetime I could feel my own heaviness and pain.

LUCY MERCER

POETRY

DREAM HOUSES

I forget
some days
in Helepolis –
chapelles
of blue peaches
call the foam-line
'Men of Rome'
my wheel emits
uncertain as
gaspereau

INVAGINATION

Had to get special curtains made for my son's – well our – room the window is so tall; blackout material behind navy blue falling between falling silver icons of starshapes and silver scythes; the whole fall of the curtain is, I realise sitting here, waiting for my son to fall asleep, exactly the same as the tent curtain drapery of *that* tent, before those stiff little velarii with their green and red socks drew them ôpen to show her, just standing there in the shocking light of the place where there is no outside, covering and covering and covering *for*

GARLANDS

Was given a garland of grama grass,
lark, use this folded grama to shelter your chicks,
like these purple bells of foxgloves
dried into slips of circles like bruises,
seeking wind, do not vex us with your branches –

Eurus (the east wind) comes down to touch
a little brown-and-red kite having eaten so much –
'O mother, my guts are spilling out of my mouth'

SPAR

A mother should never be waiting.
I water the opaque gum berg by
Twelve numbers of fake clock fire sparkling
Like garage tinsel – made to mystify.
We only know ourselves in spar-light
Disappointments. The hurt self defends
Itself – glass shivers, our faces near –
DVDs knocked like snow to every end.
Cunningly weaving snow into ourselves
For no relief of wanting (of what?)...
My mind looks through half-known-used shelves
While half-frozen assistants are sat
Like bored angels waiting for the Just –
How will this wanting be, without us? *Penelope*

WINTER STABLES

If you wanna come to my place then, we can talk about the weather – Litany

Come peep at this picture of a mother horse & her child
pony. She, a cloud, is begging, *I don't want to die again,*
I don't want to die again - silently as a glassblower
as he rests, warm and content as Sunday dinner
in the crook of her neck, the snowed-on
roof of which extends over him to his tail.
Her ears are up in the invadosphere: mouth
sounds of two 'sleeping' dogs
lying on their taken-off cheetah costumes to hide them,
Two others whispering behind dried out palm leaves.
Sometimes she's there, sometimes she's just
her shape. Ω Glows erasure as it expands –
A birth always begins with the end of
a mother, spring...
Snow to wind, which is metal ribbons pulled & pulled over.

MISS MARX

Midautumn is still covering Jew's Walk with rain. The gutters dressed in the white afternoon rain, swallowing their dresses' flowing material. *Plo-t-a-plot-plot.* Very cold clair. In the margins, rows of trees are shaking. They're protesting outside the *Den,* by the bins. Indignant leaves of their brown clocks. The ligation that binds them to the passing of themselves. And at night? They sound as if they're drawing in the dark...

Dogs have been here, wet pawmarks and broken twigs. I picked up a gift here once (a 'chair') and carried it back in squalls of rain – it took, it felt, just over a hundred years. '*Were the abstractness to catch their minds their action would cease to be exchange and the abstraction would not arise.*' And you, sister Eleanor? Taking dog's acid (prussic) and lying full on your bed, feeling your own loving sutures burn away their wishful shapes in their own darkwest, unable to write your laws?

SINGLE MOTHER

I had one mother too many

The sea dropped its findings or unfastened
as two brief-lit hard parapets unfastened;
made a wild chronotope out of my body,
but now, *said Anne*, I am matronly,
my climaxes perverse in their free
zigzags of melted sutures, these stiff fingers,
aliens of no beginning, alone with me,
another evening in spent moving them
across my picturebooks: watching *Clouds*
dream spray and spray across the silver ss
ssealed sea

*

Fell into the matricene *h*our problematic
ten thousand years of thorny overwhelmed
mothers flighted spinning in such spheres of fright,
mothers repeating *Polly-Polly-Poly-glot,*
mothers sealing ears with moly the plant,
mothers levering scabs on legs earliest of the sofa,
mothers plucking hairs like shot birds
preparing themselves no eschatologies Ω

CEMETIERE MARIN

Two mismatching 'Classical' angels in stone; the smaller points her mould-finger to the sky ringing its blue phones; hundreds of sweating horses in royal blue saddles running in a complete blur; trees break into images on the long-collapsing dusty stone; and the other? everyone wants to be the same when they're dead – crosses and angels of stone; rigid!; as though one torso on another were the lace of the same palm tree; though even the single grass is full of that complicated history; whose mouth is this close underneath? I'm sure their beauty would surprise me, though I could not understand it; my phone flickers in its awful irreal; katabasis of a face wrought in sunlight;

Katabasis of willow-pollen turning the street margins into sand with bright dust; the truth is I am afraid of being left alone in pain; *I am sorry you are all dead but I am not dead; I am half-asleep*; I have delicate hands like a statue of a woman in recline; when I am old they will be swollen in recline; I hold them like filigree against my face as I lie down on this stone that is not a page; *I am sorry for trying to disturb you as you are not disturbed*; the pupil gathers her images in her suspension tank; a woman wrapped in sparkling blue clouds turns me pop song blue too; *have I told you lately I love you*; such sea rushing over this yellow-green scrub; oh hundreds of floating green sandals of grass——

LETTER 3

Walking home two coronas in one hand
(feet repeating in a track)
late-night sky seems pinkish as it has of late –
bem! even tho world is horrible right now
I think of you ringing me in the bare library, hiding from
your wife, and god, it makes me happy? – (& *how we like to talk about god!*)
oh set unsettling. but sky – record of records –
is pinkish & *The Essential Dean Martin* is on!
my imaginary is suddenly of corded phones
of looping, chewable plastic;
'I love to be adored' – me too – you too –
these two bottles clink like crowns.
more & more in my life, L.,
I feel like Everything Has A Recognising Tendency
my friends: I'm sure I've been with them before—
my analyst: 'souls! – what they tell you these days
you don't have them?'
me: 'no – it's all quite a discovery...'
what you remember
what you don't
what you don't want to remember...
yesterday on *Antiques Roadshow* a woman displayed
a painting of a white missionary church in an Amazon jungle,
she loved its naiveté – those missionaries
in their softbrush world – helping, kind missionaries!
I abhor her...
(but not the idea of being a convertee...)
& I didn't say on the phone
my next door neighbours speak glossolalia at 3am
they're speaking your bad confused magical memories
(hope you don't hear them when we fuck)
you see, you & I, fleur-de-lis-
are complicated, and weird – (*what an editing tendency we have*)
'the Brazilian diplomat' is a metaphor. maybe it's all a metaphor –
& I had a horrible dream
I was devoured by a spirit – I told you –
lifesize, o absolute terror, eaten by my own spirit,
translucent & malicious dripping
indiscriminate dragon and woke up screaming –
I don't want to be alone (*I do*). I think maybe I don't want to be alone (*I do*)
  if you're near.

ROSSALIA

The son turns his sleeping ear towards me
scarlet from fever,
How the thermometer's light goes
from one ear to the other blindly –
in turn, I cannot tell this face as
it appears attending, only
write as light soundlessly in the ear
seeking the structure of things without respite.
In The Palace of Dreams of the Red Siècle
crimson angels and knights doze (but oh
so cautiously) in their plush pink niches
as the conversation inside the great hall goes
anxiously on, *marmor marmor marmor* –
My son, we have given you our two
'priscae gentilitatis obsoletum errorem' –
two old and outmoded pagan
understandings.
And now you are asleep, I am fearfully
examining them with this little battery light –

ANDREA BÜTTNER

Andrea Büttner is a German artist and researcher living and working in Berlin and London. In 2017 Büttner was nominated for the Turner Prize for exhibitions at Kunst Halle St. Gallen and David Kordansky Gallery Los Angeles, in which she presented a series of woodcuts based upon the German Expressionist Ernst Barlach's sculpture *Veiled Beggar* (1919) as well as etchings made by enlarging the smeared traces of fingerprints found on a smartphone screen.

Her practice often involves working in archives and bringing marginal historical collections to light for contemporary viewers. Her 2014 installation *Hidden Marriages: Gwen John and Moss* at the National Museum of Cardiff placed moss samples alongside lesser-known drawings by John found in the museum's collection. For the series *Painted Stones* (2017) Büttner searched through museum collections and auction house databases for examples of small stones or pebbles painted by artists, across various histories. Included among them are painted limestone from the Late Palaeolithic Age, a pebble with Christ on a cross by Salvador Dali, mask-like stones by Pablo Picasso and Le Corbusier, little stone assemblages by Kurt Schwitters, and a lumpen, wrinkled face by Princess Fahrelnissa Zeid. Büttner took photographs of these artefacts as they appeared on her computer screen, and adjusted the dimensions so that each stone appears as life-size.

PLATES

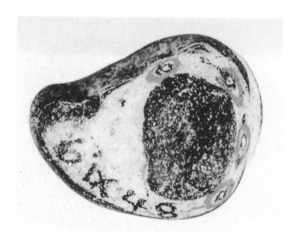

DANEZ SMITH   INTERVIEW

I met Danez Smith in Manchester at the end of January 2018, before their event at the Anthony Burgess Centre. Smith's collection *Don't Call Us Dead* had just been published in the UK, having already appeared in the US to much acclaim, including a shortlisting for the National Book Award in Poetry. But Smith's work (their latest, their 2014 debut *[insert] boy*, and two pamphlets of poems, *hands on your knees* and *black movie*) has not only been praised by reviewers and critics. Smith's reputation is founded initially in live performance; their transatlantic visibility precedes them through a variety of online and print platforms as well as a huge social media following, all of which has created a community of poets and readers, something central to both their writing and live performance. Smith grew up in St Paul, Minnesota and became a fixture of the slam poetry scene – they are a 2011 Individual World Poetry Slam finalist and reigning two-time Rustbelt Individual Champion, as well as festival director for the Brave New Voices International Youth Poetry Slam. Smith currently co-hosts the popular Poetry Foundation podcast, VS. It is no surprise that Smith's onstage charisma and passion exudes from work that is rooted both in the personal and in a community that extends well beyond their experiences as a black, queer American poet wrestling with a national legacy of violence.

As the event's host, the poet Andrew McMillan, commented during the Q&A later that evening, from this side of the Atlantic it feels as though American poetry is going through a golden age: American poets (especially poets of colour) are fuelling a political collective consciousness and discourse around identity and equality. Smith is grateful for a British audience while also being humbly cautious about taking the spotlight from a UK poet of colour. They, like a number of Black American poets from Amiri Baraka to Claudia Rankine, are part of a crucial transatlantic conversation that must continue to converge as nativist rhetoric rages in both the US and the UK.

Smith begins their reading that evening by pointing out that any white British person in the audience who thinks they can exempt themselves from the horror of America's racial violence is plainly wrong: the British 'invented racism'. Certainly the American legacy of racism owes a lot to the British Empire, whose descendants Smith suggests would prefer to spectate, aghast, at the crimes of their former colony. Of course, the mostly white crowd sitting in this room are not the ones that need convincing; one hopes that they will do more than merely acknowledge their privilege. Smith moves the audience to act, to laugh, applaud, respond, snap their fingers (some do) and interact with their voice on the stage. Momentarily, we become plural in the act of listening – a rare spirit of communalism against a shared pain rears up and dissipates, leaving us with a renewed sense of purpose. What Smith's work gives us is an unwavering sense of responsibility for the survival of others and ourselves.   SANDEEP PARMAR

TWR   Now that your book has been published in the UK, I wanted to begin by asking you about any differences you sense between UK and US poetry readerships. How prepared do you feel for a UK audience?

DS   I haven't actually thought about it too much. My allegiances are to the poem and to the people who inhabit my poems, so while I've been very excited about the UK release of my book, I haven't paid much mind to the readers it might find here. If I had a different job, I might prepare differently for a British audience, but luckily my job is to be a poet, and poetry is less interested in borders than people are. I say all that to say that I 'prepared' by being the poet and person I am. I sort of wonder about the white British person's experience reading my poetry, and I think a lot of them will probably excuse themselves from a lot of the indictments that I have in my book. I think the British people like to fancy themselves as being less racist than their American cousins, which is complete bullshit. So I also hope they'll be able to see themselves and not just the Americanness I'm indicting in the book, and I hope we can have some honest and good conversations.

TWR   As you'll know, there's a transatlantic conversation happening around poets of colour, or BAME poets as we call them in the UK, and the ways in which their work is perceived against a kind of white, predominately lyric mainstream style. Thinking about your own experiences in the US with writing organisations, communities and collectives like Cave Canem, do you have any sense of similar emerging communities for People of Colour here in the UK?

DS   On past visits to the UK, I've been able to meet with Dub poets in Manchester and the spoken word organisation Apples and Snakes in London. There are a lot of amazing poets of colour here. But Britain feels too far behind the US in terms of celebrating their poets of colour. When you look at the T.S. Eliot Prize in the past year, which I'm so glad that Ocean Vuong won, I think it's ridiculous that Vuong was the *only* poet of colour on that list and that the only poet of colour on that list was coming from America. It's ridiculous to me that Kayo Chingonyi's collection wasn't nominated, that many other collections by POC writers weren't up there. And I have a sense of hesitancy around my own book. While I do hope that the book does well here, I also hope that

my doing well doesn't 'take a spot' from a British poet of colour. Poets of colour here are doing a lot of interesting, inventive work and I think POCs understand the dangers of individualism, so we tend to collectivise in the interests of community just because that's how we're raised and how we survive. So I'd be interested to hear how British poets of colour are already finding themselves collectivising, who they recognise as their pillars and advocates.

TWR   Do you think that the publishing industry, and problems of canon-formation, will change?

DS   I think it is going to change. I think there are a lot of poets of colour who realise that there are other places to go besides academia in terms of where our work lives. And I think the imagined audience for poetry is broadening. I don't know how much mind I pay to canon-formation. All our canons are personal. What reading many reviews of POC poets by often white reviewers in the States has shown me is that there is a clear dissidence between what folks consider canonical. Often my poems are talked about in relation to a canon that couldn't be further from my mind or my heart. I also very much think that we need more POC critics, reviewers, folks who are able to actually speak to the lineage, the trends and the cultures that exist in the art to be able to get down to the craft of the work. When I see a lot of white critics reviewing books by poets of colour, they're actually reviewing the culture. They're reviewing the funk of the poem but they're not actually able to talk about it in the sense of the lyric or the line, all the amazing things POC poets are pushing and inventing in terms of craft. They're actually just amazed at the brownness of the stories. That has to change. We need folks who can actually hold the work to be able to shout it to the mountaintops and properly critique it.

TWR   How does your poetics respond to your background in performance?

DS   For me, it's about writing a good poem. The questions of page and performance come later. My first allegiance is with what the poem wants to be, in terms of how it looks. The question of performance is something I ask myself at a later date once the poem is finished, when I ask myself, 'can I read this to an audience one time through and be able to make them feel something?' Some poems are just easier to translate to a space of performance than others. While I do consider myself a performer, at this point in my career I don't think I enter into a poem seeking to write a performance piece. I think I very much used to, but right now I'm just trying to write good work. I think what I carry over from performance is a sense of *duende* – doing a thing with feeling. And I never want an audience – whether they are holding my work in their hands and taking it in with their eyes or whether my body is present and I'm able to give it to them through their ears – I never want them to feel the same at the beginning of a poem as they do at the end. I never want someone to leave my poems bored.

TWR   Tell me a little bit about how your earlier chapbook, *Black Movie*, from which some poems appear in *Don't Call Us Dead*, relates to the visibility or spectacle of black bodies in media, folklore and other cultural and social spaces.

DS   *Black Movie* is a catalogue of how I was feeling at the start of the Black Lives Matter movement in the United States. I think of Black Lives Matter as being not only a direct result of police violence but of how black death became an obsession in American mass media. It wasn't that we hadn't been being killed or weren't dying or that police violence had lessened in the years prior, but rather American media decided to turn its attention to police brutality once again in 2013 and 2014. So I really just wanted to capture that moment and what it was like to feel that black death was inescapable both on the TV, via social media, and all these ways in which we were being bombarded by images of black death, while also capturing the depressingness of how that was calling toward a kind of justice that we'd been waiting for for a long time. Because while cases like Trayvon Martin and Michael Brown felt very harsh, in our mindset if you are Black American you knew that those stories were not new and that they had been happening since forever.

Also, I think in order to write about such harsh topics there has to be an element of play. For any author to be able to delve into depressing or hard topics you need something, and so this idea of films, these sort of mini-movies, this idea of image-making, was a tether that I used to help myself buoy into the work. Because without that construction of thinking about, 'how do I frame this in a thematic kind of way towards this thing I'm building?', I would have really lost myself in the work and not been able to do what I did.

TWR   Thinking more about the spectacle of black death, I'd like to ask you about the poem 'Short Film' that is expanded in *Don't Call Us Dead* and retitled 'not an elegy'. Elsewhere, in 'the politics of elegy', you write about a (presumably white) woman who tells you that she really enjoys your work and how strange that is, given the subject matter. How does elegy function within the spectacle?

DS   The elegy is such an intimate form, and I needed to recognise the lack of intimacy that I actually had with these people. What happens with the spectacle of death is that it makes you know a person without actually knowing them. To only know a person because of their death is something different to being able to really celebrate the life, which is what I think an elegy should be able to do. It should allow someone in death access to a moment of their living. But I didn't actually know the texture of these people's living, so I was only able to love someone because of their victimhood. So 'not an elegy' allows a respectful distance, and in a poem like 'summer, somewhere' I'm trying to recognise that distance.

I also wanted to recognise the weirdness of what capitalism does to the making of art. I know that, for me, I felt insecure because a lot of the beginnings of my recognition in the poetry scene were attached to these poems about black death. So even though I was writing a wide range of work on a plethora of topics, it was 'dear white america', 'not an elegy' and 'alternate names for black boys', all these poems that are thinking directly about black death, that propelled my name into the American consciousness in poetry. That then meant that I could become a full-time artist and be doing all these shows and all of a sudden I had money in my pocket because of poetry. That was weird, and I had to deal with that, and I didn't know how to. So I think 'politics of elegy' and 'not an elegy' is a way of recognising the muckiness of that. And, thinking about 'Short Film', I remove all the names when it becomes 'not an elegy', and that is to speak to the haphazardness of black death and police brutality and how it could be anyone. So I was really purposeful about removing those names and trying to let it be known that this list is ever-evolving. This applies to more than just the individual black person that we can point to and know, but is a continuous story that we need to address.

TWR   Listing and the erasure of names leads me to the final poem of the book, where there's an apocalyptic image of black people standing on the shoreline interrogating the ocean which has swallowed their ancestors. Here naming, or calling, offers a moment of hope which is quite beautiful.
DS   Naming is important. In many black cultures you learn the importance of giving the right name or not naming things. So I try to be purposeful in *Don't Call Us Dead* about where we get a name and also what types of names we use, right? So even that title, 'don't call us dead', is followed by the line 'call us alive someplace better'. It recognises that we can't remove ourselves from sorrow, but we can reframe it. We can do it in a way that isn't commodifying or objectifying these new ancestors we now have, who have been created out of systems of oppression and white supremacy. I like naming things, and I think what happens with naming is that it brings me closer to the work and it helps me to not make puppets out of my subjects, both when I'm writing about other folks and when I'm writing about myself. Because the book is very much about my diagnosis with HIV, which made me a very sad boy when I was writing, but one thing I never want to do is to feel like I'm masking myself or who I'm talking about in writing. So that act of naming brings it sort of blood-close.

TWR   Your poem 'alternate names for black boys' from *[insert] boy* brings me to my next question, about the general name 'boy', which you use quite often in different ways. What does 'boy' mean to you?
DS   I like the word 'boy' a lot because 'boy' is a messy term and I like messy things. I like all the racial and sexual complications of a word like 'boy'. Many folks feel a certain way seeing a black male body or person use a word like 'boy' in their work, because they immediately go to a repressive American society in which 'boy' is a term of disrespect used to keep a black man in place. Sure, that can be there as well, but it's never the way in which I use it. For me, 'boy' comes from a reclaimed sense of the word. This is close to my feelings about the N-word as well. At least in terms of the more racially focussed poems, when I say 'boy' it's to say something about kinship and to say something about friendship. To say 'that's my boy' is to say that is my friend, that is my brother. And then in

the sexual sense I think I'm very much interested in boyness, in how it relates to being a sub, how it relates to acts of submission and domination. But also there's something too final and unimaginative about adulthood to me. 'Man' just feels like a very boring and final act, or a very boring object to be, whereas 'boy' allows it to be closer to childhood, which for me gives the poems more access to wonder and fantasy and magical realism and surrealism, so it feels like I can be stranger as a boy than I can be as a man. So I feel that even as old as I am now, and I'm not that old, I still feel a little attached to boyness in the work. And boys are allowed to be soft, too.

TWR   In your poem 'everyday is a funeral & a miracle' you write 'anything is possible in a place / where you can burn a body / with less outrage than a flag'. Do you feel optimistic about poetry as a way to allow modern-day Americans to reflect on their national identities?
DS   I feel very optimistic and pessimistic at the exact same time. I think those that know to come to poetry have already started receiving the salve that poetry has to offer. I think it is very hard to be a fan of poetry and also to be a closed-hearted individual. And I'm fascinated by people who are. [Laughs] There's something about the form of poetry that brings us closer to our own humanness or humanity in a very real way. Maybe it's something to do with the brevity, maybe it's something about the lyric, I don't know. I think poems are both songs and spells, and I think both have the ability to open you up. So I'm very optimistic about the current state of American poetry. There's a celebration of stories that have not been celebrated for too long. We're seeing more immigrant narratives, more POC narratives and queer and trans narratives, that are not just being published but are popular. Fans of American poetry are becoming better citizens of their country because they are citizens of the genre.

But I'm also pessimistic because I think it's very easy to shut poetry out – a lot of times we're just preaching to the choir. I would assume Trump voters have never read a poem, or they're reading older stuff and aren't able to engage with contemporary work. I wonder, what is the art of a racist? I don't really know and I don't want to find out. So I'm optimistic that those who are already part of the good church of poetry will continue to get better, but I'm pessimistic about those who need most to be able to find it. I think what's happening, especially under our current administration, is that we seem to be confused about what a fact is, what an opinion is and what a truth is. So I am wondering if the divisions in all the Americas that exist are becoming so wide that we are approaching a point of sea-change, which I'm happy about because I think things in America will have to get very, very ugly before they start to get better. There are a lot of uncomfortable conversations and truths and possible violences that we're going to have to face up to before we are going to be actually able to do the good work of change.

TWR   You connect the lyric with human experience and an emotional (and political) connection with readers. Thinking about some of the recent debates in anti-lyric or avant-garde poetry, in particular by poets of colour (like Cathy Park Hong, Evie Shockley and many others), how might anti-lyric poets fit into your view of poetry? Your work is sometimes formal and other times there's an expanded, liberated sense of where the 'I' sits. What might some of the ethical questions be around the lyric?

DS   When I say lyric I'm not talking about what lyric has traditionally been seen as. For me, lyric is really a question of code: who is speaking, who are they speaking to and what are they trying to say and how do they want the reader to feel about it? And I don't attach much to this idea of the 'lyric I' being this detached voice that is speaking into space. For some reason that's always felt very white to me. I think that only white authors have had the privilege of not having their bodies considered in their work. The lyric has always privileged a particular kind of voice, when to me everything is a kind of lyric, whether it's high lyric or low lyric (I'm interested in low lyric, too). Things that are plainly spoken or colloquial can also be to me a type of lyric, not just in the rhythm but in who is called into the work because of how the work is written. That's really what the lyric is about for me. Everything I do is lyric – and lyrics for whom. Maybe I attach it too closely to song lyrics as well; being a student of hip-hop, I know there are so many codes in hip-hop. Kendrick Lamar will write a verse in a particular kind of way depending on who he wants to speak to and he knows that he's alienating some folks sometimes, and I love that. Because he's talking to his people. Or when he's not talking to his people it's clear when he's talking to

a white audience. The lyric is just a set of keys that every poet sort of agrees on about what doors are going to open through their words.

I don't always know what folks mean when they say the avant-garde. We can have awesome strangeness and at the same time be interested in accessibility. We can be who we want and we can say it how we want. I want folks to know what it is I'm talking about because I'm talking to these very urgent things: that's just the sort of poet I was raised to be. My first interactions with poetry were through spoken word. I was raised in the school of thinking about the personal narrative in the work, telling the stories of yourself and your communities, so that is the work that I tend to do. It's not interested in hiding. There are poets who are very dear to me who are, I think, considered part of the avant-garde, but I think we slip in and out of that so much. The term 'avant-garde', and even 'experimental', is very dangerous in poetry, because usually it's a term that folks run away from. But I think those words also give us permission to access our strangeness, so they can be very beautiful.

The avant-garde and conceptual poetry gets a really bad name because of folks like Kenneth Goldsmith and Vanessa Place. When I think of the avant-garde I think of the work of Lillian-Yvonne Bertram, Robin Coste Lewis, Franny Choi or Harryette Mullen, who is also saying some wild urgent shit in her work. I think some of Terrance Hayes's poems are definitely living in the world of the avant-garde. Tyehimba Jess – *Olio* is one of the most avant-garde pieces that I think I've ever read. It is a big, crazy, experimental, uncategorisable book of poetry. Nate Mackey, Duriel Harris. All these folks who are doing amazing work but who are not part of that same white-tent school of the avant-garde people tend to talk about. What this is all to say is that I want to divorce the idea of the lyric as something that is ascribed to certain types of voices or certain styles of writing. The question is more: what is this person's lyric? How does this poet sing? Every poet has to answer that for themselves.

TWR   I want to ask you about the ghosts that appear quite regularly throughout your work, as haunting or as shadows of the self.

DS   The ghost has always been a language that I've known how to speak just from my background; I'm very much raised in a Southern Baptist tradition. So the idea of the ghost in that realm being the Holy Ghost is something that has always been real to me. Growing up in church I would see women and men jumping up, hollering, spinning around and falling because they were 'caught in the ghost'. Also from a very paranormal sense, I grew up in a haunted house – I don't know who died but there's at least two ghosts in my grandmother's house. And my grandfather is a newer ghost: he died there, so I can still go in there and feel him. They've never been bad ghosts. All the ghosts in my house have been good. So ghosts have always been very much real and the afterlife is something I've been thinking a lot about, as well as the idea of how we can all become ghosts within ourselves, too.

To be queer has for a long time been to be a ghost in our society. I think queer folks are just now learning how to be fully alive in public, and alive at all times in a new way that has only been possible in recent years – and to be so without fear. Through my own experience I know that my queerness is very different from that of my queer ancestors. When I go to high schools and junior highs in America right now, kids are way more out and way more sure and way more elegant with the language they use to describe themselves and their orientations and their genders than we ever were. So queerness is alive in the world in a very different way. In a way that is allowing folks to no longer feel like ghosts in their own bodies. Ghost is a useful term to talk about who is allowed to be alive in our world, who is allowed to be fully alive. In *Don't Call Us Dead*, there's a discussion about the HIV community, which includes a lot of ghosts. You can't talk about HIV in the queer community without talking about who is absent. Also talking about police violence in the black community, talking about victims of police brutality or white supremacy as a whole (it doesn't always have to be police) is talking about who's not there. It's also a form of respect when you come from a culture that respects its ancestors, a culture that has that memory of who got you here, who might not be physically at the table. You learn how to respect and honour ghosts in a different way.

TWR   I want to ask you about a couple of lines from '1 in 2', that are prefaced by the statistic that one in two black men who have sex with men will be diagnosed with HIV in their lifetime. You write, 'if you trace the word *diagnosis*, back enough / you'll find *destiny* // trace it forward, find

diaspora.' Destiny, diagnosis, diaspora. Tell me more about the connection between those things.
DS   It's really hard for me to think of myself as an individual, because I've always imagined myself in a community. I think for myself and for a lot of poets of colour there is always a 'we' folded in behind the 'I'. So these ideas about what is an individual destiny versus what is a symptom of your community become very much blurred. And this is the subtle thing about whiteness, that's where the idea of meritocracy comes from, is that white folks are able to think of themselves as pulling themselves up by their bootstraps – Donald Trump calling himself a self-made millionaire even though his father gave him a million-dollar loan and many bailouts. So I think that idea of diagnosis as something we can both trace in an individual sense of destiny but also the communal sense of diaspora; how we imagine ourselves within that is also to recognise the many genocides we go through. But also our celebrations, too. That line isolated feels a little different. Within the context of the poem it's sad as heck. But we can also use that line to think about our communal victories as well. How we can imagine ourselves into possible utopias as well as how our individual effort can be for communal gain.

TWR   I want to move on to talk about joy and passion and desire, which all run through your work. One of the criticisms of the lyric is that because of its emotional immediacy it has become a readily consumable commodity. It fits into an economy of pleasure that is so predictable that it's like taking an addictive hit, which in the modern world is facilitated through social media, sex / dating apps, the things you discuss in your poems. We're told that momentary joy via technology wards off profound modern loneliness. But there's also a bit of dark anonymity and moments of violence here, alongside joy. How do these balance in the modern world as you experience it?
DS   It would be dishonest to write about a modern gay male experience without speaking to how our sex is attached to our technologies. It's a modern fact about our relationships that we cannot divorce our desire from our Wi-Fi. I'm trying to talk about the use of code in technology and code in language and what is lost or muddled or even pixelated and therefore blurred in our relationships and desires with these technological advances. This is just what it means to be a queer person

who has sex in the new millennium. The ways we find each other have greatly changed. It's not as cruisey any more, it's not men walking around parks or going to these very specific spaces looking for certain handkerchiefs that folks wear in order to code themselves. I could hop on my phone and within a three-mile radius I can know how many men I can have access to, them and their bodies. I don't think I'm trying to say anything in particular when talking about technology, but I am saying I'm a queer of my times, which means I have some thoughts about Grindr.

TWR   It's interesting that you are wanting to be honest about modernity and your relationship to technology, as a queer person in particular. Honesty and authenticity seem to be part of your aim as a poet as well. And yet fantasy and passion are attachable to versions of the self in your work, too. Some of these poems address being made anonymous by something like a dating app. To a certain extent poetry and especially the lyric is also a means of presenting inauthentic selves, isn't it? For example, in 'strange dowry' anonymity becomes a recognition which leads to a kind of intimacy that is replaced finally by the mundane, the everyday. Is that a bit like the relationships poets develop with their readers?

DS   I think so. I think any poet worth their salt is trying to show the full picture for their reader. And that's why you can have a poem like that, which moves through these sort of lyrical interesting moments to these very mundane moments talking about email. I think with poetry you want it to feel unstable in a particular kind of way. You want to be able to zoom in and out as fast as possible, where the reader can be taken from looking at the scope of the world to a crack in a street corner. Part of the vulnerability of a poet is both how we make ourselves fantastic and impossible and also tangible and small to our readers at the same time, which is what I think they want. When I'm a reader I want to feel like the poet is both godlike and just as human as me. That's our agreement with the reader, to be our fully naked selves but also to show them something they've never seen before, to take off our mask and be another kind of creature. I'm not trying to hide behind a version of the lyric 'I'; the 'I' in my poems is always me or is always 85 per cent me, or many versions of myself combined into one. That's because poems have the ability to be 'True' or sometimes just 'true'. I'm trying to write poems that say, 'Hey reader, you can trust me because I first had to be honest with myself in order to write this.'

TWR   What are you working on now?

DS   I'm working on a lot of things now. Some of them are outside the realm of writing. By the end of this year I really hope to be doing stand-up more, which is something I used to do that I want to dive back into again to access a different part of my creative brain. As for writing, I'm working on a novel that involves time-travel. It's about relationships and death. There's a woman who chooses to time-travel in order to save her child and live a life with her child again. But what that means is that, while she goes off and has what she hopes is her perfect family with her husband and her now not-dead-anymore child, she's no longer present in her other timeline. In the future her husband is left with the dead child and a wife that left him to go be with that child and another version of him. So we kind of follow these two timelines in which a lot of things happen. It starts to call into question what things are destiny, what should we allow to happen and different relationships to intimacy – but I won't give away too much. It's my first jaunt into fiction.

Finally, a third poetry collection will be out in the States in 2020. That has two titles, one is *Homey* and one is *My Nig*. I think *My Nig* is a truer title, I just don't want white folks saying *My Nig* when they talk about my book. But I think it's the book where I'm least considering white people in my work. For a while I was struggling with this question of what do you do with the white gaze, can we get rid of it, and then I just had to listen to a lot of my black and POC mentors who said don't consider it and I was like, oh yeah, I guess it is just that easy. And so it's a book for my friends, it's a book about friendship and about many kinds of friendships and intimacy, and about living and about suicide and about loss and worship and all these other things. So it's a book near and dear to my heart. I think a lot of my work is about rethinking a familial type of intimacy, both across the novel, the poetry collection and the jokes that are forming in the stand-up, too.

S. P.,
Manchester, January 2018

REALLY TECHNO
JULIA BELL

ESSAY

'Ich bin einer,' I say when my turn comes. *I am one.*

I've been here before, outside this colossal power station in Friedrichshain, just over the Spree in the old East, very near to where the Berlin Wall once stood. On previous occasions I queued with friends, the first time for three hours on a balmy Saturday night, which also happened to be the club's birthday party. I got in just as the sun was coming up. The second time for forty minutes in midwinter, the temperature a bone-throbbing -11. Today I'm acting like a Berliner and doing it solo on an indifferent Sunday in April.

I'm not here to take drugs, or get drunk, I'm not really looking to hook up; in fact, once I get in, if you dance too close to me I'll probably move. I'm here as a 45-year-old woman, to be on my own, surrounded by techno music played on one of the best sound systems in the world, the harder and louder the better.

The building towers over us, monolithic concrete and steel, graffiti covering the bottom floors. It's getting on for 3 p.m. and there's about a half-hour queue leading up to the entrance. Most of them are male: one mixed group of hopeful tourists who get refused; two thickly bearded men who have obviously spent last night hooking up with each other. They have the kinetics of recent sex in the way they touch each other and shimmy to the muffled beat, which gets louder as we approach the door. In the final few metres nobody speaks. We're within range of the bouncers now and according to the websites that give advice on how to get in, drawing attention to yourself by being too loud will get you turned away.

There's a whole mythology of cool around getting into this place, especially among 20-something corporate types and curious tourists. One time I saw a couple who looked like they'd emerged from a *Vogue* photo shoot, or a private yacht party, or both – nuclear suntans and white linens, dazzling teeth, expensive gold jewellery – children of the hyper wealthy – arguing petulantly with the bouncers because they'd been refused.

This isn't a club for the beautiful people, although there are many beautiful people inside. It's a place that emerged from the East German queer punk scene, and what that couple didn't realise in their moneyed armour was that the door policy exists expressly to keep them out. To stop the club being colonised by tourists: becoming some idea of the sleek life like the Buddha Bar, or Nobu, or the terraces of Ibiza or some other high fashion hangout where the atmosphere is like a cross between a wake and a self-conscious teenage disco; where everyone watches everyone else so fiercely that by the end of the evening their faces are flayed with the strain.

The name is a synthesis of two Berlin districts, which were separated by the wall, Kreuz*berg* and Freidrichs*hain*. The club itself was carved out of an old power station as big as the Turbine Hall of the Tate Modern. Sven Marquardt, the head doorman who famously turned away Britney Spears, has said that he wants people who look like they know how to party. I have only been once where he was on the door, in gold Elvis shades, his face full of piercings and tattoos; sovereign of the queue, impassive, a contemporary Captain Kurtz.

Being outside looking in evokes in me an immediate, intense longing to be inside. The experience reminds me of an art installation I stumbled across once in a field in Norwich. A shack of grey corrugated iron from inside of which emanated some very loud and crunchy hip hop. Involuntarily, my body moved. I walked around the whole structure twice before realising that there was, deliberately, obviously, no door.

Queuing for Berghain is a bit like this, or rather, like being part of
a mass performance art piece which enacts purgatory. For some, just to
have stood in the queue is enough, even if it means they have presented
themselves to be turned away.

I'm close enough now to see the faces of the bouncers. They are turning away a group of young Berliners in front of me who've jumped the
queue, and a lone girl from Glasgow with her pineapple hair and stone-
washed denim who told me she read about the place in a magazine. I'm in
a black hoodie and jeans. I'm nothing glitzy or special. There is a terrible
suspended pause and then it's my turn.

I look him in the eye and fight a sudden urge to yawn.

The bouncer smiles. 'How many times have you been here?' he asks in
English.

I wonder what to say. None, many, a few. I wonder if I should lie.
I know I'm showing my age. At 45 I look lived-in these days. Perhaps
I should know better. Now I am entering middle age I should know my
place, and restrict my public dancing to the occasional house party where,
if I'm lucky, after too many glasses of Prosecco someone will spin me
round to something with a Nile Rogers bassline and my heels will get
stuck in the carpet.

I came to Berlin partly to escape this, which is, like a lot of things,
more pronounced in the UK than in Europe. Single, still strong, childfree,
I have a freedom and a flexibility unavailable to many women my age. My
childfree status is my liberation, but it also puts me out of time with some
of my peers, and the general, oppressive, conservative narrative of what
we should be doing when. Especially as a woman, and even more especially as a queer woman.

Judith, now Jack Halberstam and others have argued that it is not our
sex acts which constitute queerness, but rather what we do with our time.
S/he suggests that we 'try to think about queerness as an outcome of
strange temporalities, imaginative life schedules, and eccentric economic
practices', so that we can 'detach queerness from sexual identity and come
closer to understanding Foucault's comment in *Friendship as a Way of Life*
that "homosexuality threatens people as a 'way of life' rather than as a
way of having sex."

This is what the many – hilarious – websites which obsess about how
to get into Berghain don't get: this is primarily a queer club. And you can't
really pretend to be queer. Perhaps it's something you can become, but
mostly it's something you just are.

In the end I say nothing. The bouncer nods me in. And as always,
the ego lifts.

The first thing to happen once I'm over the threshold is the tricky business of my phone. Before the bag search they take my smartphone and
put a sticker over the camera lens and another on the screen to prevent
me taking selfies. If they find you taking pictures they'll throw you out.
This one simple restriction creates an immediate shift in the atmosphere.
No one is watching, or rather, no one is watching themselves watching
the party. What happens in Berghain stays in Berghain. A quick search
on Instagram under #Berghain reveals mostly pictures from the queue.
Once inside, the space is liberated from the shadow world of social media,
except as a means of telling your friends where you are. People who take
their phones out for longer than a moment are frowned on and it shows.
In all the corners, chill-out rooms and in the garden, people are actually
talking to each other. The only network you need is inside the club.

Once I've paid my €16 and had my arm stamped, I walk around the corner into the lobby. There are people in various stages of their experience. Some are lolled out over the banquettes, pale and jaded, ready to go home. Someone is asleep. Others are waiting for friends, or just arrived, a little dazed like me, still trying to navigate the transition between outside and in.

I queue for the Garderobe to hand in my stuff. I've come prepared. In my bag a change of clothes, a clean shirt, sunglasses, chewing gum, lip balm. I need to separate what I need now and later. Many others are doing the same. I see one of my neighbours in front of me in the queue. She's Italian and in her twenties and came to Berlin for the music scene and to get away from the economic stagnation in Italy. She greets me with a sweaty hug. She's changing her shoes because she's been here since it opened. Guest list. I think she's dating one of the DJs. She tells me I got here just in time. Len Faki has just started, to be followed by Ben Klock. Two of Berghain's most popular resident DJs. She's already twitching to the beat, hyper, pupils like moons.

'Enjoy.' She dances off and blows me a kiss.

The music from upstairs is louder, people around me are bouncing to it. At the Garderobe they sell earplugs and t-shirts with images of the stacks of black Funktion One speakers, which are making the noise upstairs. When they were installed they were the most expensive club sound system in the world.

All sounds are compression waves – they create waves of pressure in the fabric of the physical world. The most powerful can move solid objects, burst your eardrums or shatter glass. This is partly how explosions work.

The human ear has more neural connections to the brain than the eye. It can hear in a range between 20 Hz all the way up to 20,000 Hz – something like ten octaves of sound. Through a combination of deep physics and deep listening, good engineers understand how to direct and construct sound so that it can amplify across a whole stadium without distorting, or create the huge, cathedral sound of Berghain while still allowing clubbers to speak to each other on the dance floor without shouting. Even on club nights the sound is only at 10-20 per cent of its capacity, otherwise the physical experience of the sound would just be too exhausting.

The speakers have been positioned exactly and calibrated precisely to minimise feedback and articulate the full range of every sound. When you've come to dance it's a difference that you notice with your body. A difference between being able to hear the sound and live inside of it. If it's a bad sound the noise will be an assault to your senses, a battle between you and the feedback to get to the beat. A bad sound creates a bad atmosphere, bad tinnitus and a bad headache.

Tony Andrews, who designed the speakers, says that good sound is 'a state of meditation. If you feel yourself being pulled towards a meditative state, you know the sound is good. When it's really good, you don't know the difference between the inside of your head and the outside of your head.'

Walking up the stairs to the main room is an overwhelming sensory overload. Almost like taking a deep breath and diving underwater. The music moves through me, around me, with a terrible force. Loud and crisp and deep. The lights mirror the synaptic lightning of the rhythm, bass thudding like a heartbeat. The noise lifts me off my feet. Even if you don't like techno it's a spectacle of sound and people. And the speakers are so exquisitely calibrated that the sound is something your whole body hears. This is music as full body experience; music as drugs.

If you cut the sound and look at the shapes that people are making you would know they were dancing to techno from the angles of their bodies. It's an upright kind of dancing, almost militarised, tight punches and arm movements. There's a girl on the podium beating her arms in the air while moving her whole body in a sinuous curve, another making fronds from his fingers, dragging them through the air as if he were underwater. Dancing to techno rejects the disco values of sociability, of looking at your partners, making eye contact, for a much more individuated approach. Everyone on the dance floor is together but separate, facing the DJ booth, lost in sound and light. You dance with other people as anonymous silhouettes, maybe catching someone's eye when the break is especially ecstatic or a mix just dropped. Watching from the edges, the dance floor *heaves*, it moves as one body, like the surface of the sea.

Techno music evolved out of the broken industrial landscapes of Detroit and before that, Germany, with the Übermenschen of electronic music, Kraftwerk. Early Detroit techno pioneer Derrick May describes his music as Hi Tek Soul or 'George Clinton meets Kraftwerk in an elevator'. The music takes the rigidity of Kraftwerk's mechanistic orderliness and adds jazz rhythms. In the 80s new sounds were made possible by advances in digital technology – the Roland 303 bass synthesiser and the 808 drum machine – the rise of which coincided with a period of apocalyptic decline in the car-manufacturing heartlands of America, Chicago and Detroit.

Early Detroit techno musicians – May, Carl Craig, Jeff Mills and the influential Underground Resistance Collective – were Reagan-era militants. They found empowerment in the new underground youth movement of kids of all cultures coming together to dance to repetitive, trance-inducing beats in the empty warehouses of Detroit. The music spread to Europe: these new sounds drew people in their thousands to illegal raves, to underground car parks, fields in the middle of nowhere, abandoned warehouses, to dance for hours free of health and safety regulations, club promoters, security, police. The state's response was, at least in the UK, to act like an authoritarian parent. In the early 90s in the UK, more than a few people gathering around a stereo listening to 'repetitive beats' became a criminal offence, thanks to the 1994 Criminal Justice and Public Order Act.

But in the grime of post-wall Berlin, techno found a spiritual home. There were plenty of abandoned buildings in which to host parties and, in the post Stasi-era, a laxity of law and order meant that illegal parties, especially around the wall, weren't really policed. Spaces like Tresor, Der Bunker and E-Werk emerged along with groups like Basic Channel and techno became the soundtrack to a reunified Berlin.

Now the music has become assimilated to the point where Berghain is considered not an entertainment, but a cultural venue. It's partly a tax dodge – 7 per cent Culture tax instead of 19 per cent for Entertainment – but as a classification it now means that, in Berlin at least, dancing to techno at Berghain is considered high art.

I buy a Club Mate – a highly caffeinated yerba mate that tastes more natural than Red Bull. Around me there are a lot of people who are very high, gurning, nodding their heads to the music, talking loose and chewy to their friends.

When I was younger I used to take ecstasy when I went out dancing. My memories of these experiences are – mostly – ecstatic. Overwhelmed by a feeling of wellbeing and evanescence. Lost on the dance floor for hours. But since then I can make this happen without the drug. It's a neural turning that occurs in the brain, pathways once connected that can be recalled, recreated again and again under the right environmental stimulus. The place I can reach under the right conditions on the dance floor is spiritual.

Growing up, pop music was considered to be a gateway drug to a relationship with Satan. One of the few pop records of which my mother approved was Cliff Richard's naff classic *Why Should the Devil Have All the Good Music?* which borrows all its riffs from the (presumably Satanic) blues – claiming them back by inference for white people and for God.

At a Billy Graham rally I went to as a child in Bristol, the singing was as rousing as match day, the invitation, immediately afterwards, to give your soul to Jesus a neat trick. Build up the crowd to an ecstatic pitch through music and then provide a religious explanation for the experience. People poured down to the front to be blessed by Billy Graham, the old handsome American huckster. His charisma lay in his good looks and his ability to connect mass hysteria to the metaphysical.

It always fascinated me that a significant number of casualties from the early days of rave, individuals who blew their minds with excessive quantities of drugs, ended up in the Jesus Army. Their buses could usually be seen at the peripheries of the legal raves that emerged in the mid-90s. Often their members had had religious experiences on the dance floor and depressive ones on the comedown, but they connected their ecstatic experiences to a closeness with God, and saw in the lights and smoke a moving of the Holy Spirit. They also tried to convert others through their example of straight edge living, witnessing for Jesus in the middle of the rave. But for me they miss the point: dancing is a spiritual, not a religious experience; its mysteries are biological, psychological, deeply individual.

The sound has moved up a gear. Len Faki has changed the beat from a minimal military rhythm to something more complex. He drops a trippy break, a kind of backwards synthesiser, and the crowd cheers, the dancing accelerates. DJ sets at Berghain can last for five, six, seven hours; the DJs build with the crowd a sound journey, slower, faster, louder, softer. A good DJ can sense the energy of the crowd and pushes the sound to control their experience. Now I can sense the music as shapes around my body. I finish my drink and push through the crowds into the middle of the dance floor. I relax and give my body to the beat, and the heat rises.

A few weeks ago a friend of mine died from an inoperable brain tumour. For weeks I have carried a heavy weight of grief, a sense of life as fragile, unreal. I held his warm hand hours before they switched off the life support, the machines that kept him alive beeping their measurements into the cold hospital.

My friend was queer, always at right angles to everything, never quite fitting in. He found in Berlin a home of sorts, although everything for him was always tenuous. He was an artist, open, oversensitive, unable to hold down a job, too argumentative, too aware of the hypocrisy that underpins most labour, the centre would never hold. To some he might be marginal, but he was always a survivor. And fifty is no age to die. There was still so much he had to do, to offer. I am here for him too, to do something with the sadness that I have been carrying in my body.

It's not lost on me that there is a persistent beeping in this track that sounds like one of his machines. He was brain dead by the time I saw him, yet his body was warm, his skin glowing. The life support was keeping his body alive, even while he was dead. The scans showed a black mass where his brain activity should be. Where did he go? What is left of a human when they are still breathing but their brain is dead? This imponderable question has been bothering me for weeks.

I look into the crowd and for a heart-stopping second think I can see him coming towards me, with his boyish smile, his stories of how brilliantly he was getting on with the book we both knew he wasn't writing. His many kindnesses. Phrases, gestures, noises come back to me. Him saying 'I'll hate him til the day I die' or 'over my dead body'. Commonplaces that now seem like prophecies.

I let myself into the rhythm and my limbs move of their own accord. I don't control it. I'm not making any rehearsed moves, just letting my nervous system respond to the beat. My arms and legs and torso move as if connected to the sound, bypassing consciousness.

At some point I pass through the mirror into this uncanny, techno place. I am not aware of myself. I am at once all body and no body. I am out of time, out of language, my mind all sensation. The sound makes shapes, red, green, purple, which become like a physical building that the beat starts to build around me. The music has a kind of architecture, which I can see in my mind's eye. At this saturation, the sound creates its own spatial awareness, its own metaphysical structures. In this place I am connected to something bigger than me, a place outside the ego. The split parts of me are, for these few moments, suddenly whole.

On an atomic level, my physicality is being changed by the pressure waves coming from the speakers, from the movement of all the other humans around me. I am on the dance floor and above it at the same time. Even though I am surrounded by people I am solitary. I'm not even in a club, on a dance floor, but in some other space and time entirely. I am entering the trance.

Bjork describes it best: 'I had been away from Iceland for over a year and when I returned for New Year I stayed on top of a mountain. I went for a walk on my own and I saw the ice was thawing in the lava fields. All I could hear was the cackle of the ice, echoing over hundreds of square miles. It was pitch black, the Northern Lights were swirling around and just below them was a layer of thick cloud. I could see the lights from all the towns in my childhood mirrored in the reflection of these clouds, with the lava fields cackling below. It was really techno.'

I don't know how long I'm in there. I don't have a watch and I don't want to look at my phone, but at some point a change in the music, a tiredness in my legs, makes me stop. My body and the sound un-sync and all I can hear is noise.

I go to the upstairs bar where the music is softer – more house than techno. The space is full of people talking, some still nodding to the beat. I sit on a ledge with my back against the glass, peek out through the shutters. It's dark now, and there is a long queue stretching all the way along past the beer kiosk and beyond. My head throbs.

I look at my phone. It's 8.30 p. m. I've been dancing for about five hours straight and my body is tingling. I light a cigarette and a girl next to me asks to share it. She's from London, happy to be here.

'They've shut all the clubs in London,' she says. Which is true.

We talk about London nightlife. How spaces are smaller, further out from the centre, often temporary, always over-policed, controlled by security in high-vis jackets. You're always aware of being watched. There is still a subculture of illegal parties in some of the warehouse communities, but everything is provisional, there is no sense that the city really wants to allow nightlife of this old, urban kind. When land values are so stratospheric nothing is sacred. Too often it seems as if London is heading towards the obediently dreary capitalist street culture of somewhere like Singapore or Zurich, except with more homeless.

In return for a cigarette the girl buys me a beer. We talk for a while, shake our heads at our fear at what may come – we laugh at our own intensity, talking politics in a nightclub. When she stands to leave she kisses me before it can become a thought. She tastes of beer and chewing gum.

'Come to the dark room,' she says, holding out a hand to help me stand.

We go to a room behind the main dance floor. At first it's hard to see. There is a dim light somewhere behind me casting everything into shadow. There is a squash of bodies, mainly men. Someone is masturbating, in the middle are two men fucking and behind them a man with a woman pushed up against the wall, her expression a wide, wild, O. Techno thuds through the walls and the room has the heat of arousal. She kisses me again, this time for much longer. We press into each other, fumble with zips and buttons, touch arms, skin, fingers, lips, breasts, until we both shine with sweat and desire. I think of the huge statue of a Bacchus-like figure holding a giant cornucopia in the lobby by the Garderobe. Sex is the logical extension of the energy being raised on the dance floor; in this place we are all Maenad.

Afterwards, we emerge on the dance floor, blinking, as if into daylight. We catch another beat, start to dance. The hairs on my arms thicken and prickle as another acid break ripples through the crowd. The dancing gets harder and again, I am in thrall of the beat.

I lose the girl from London, find her again later in the queue for the Garderobe. It's now well after midnight and I'm done. I feel as if someone has taken me apart and not-so-subtly rearranged me. Not bad for two Club Mates and a beer. We hug goodbye, kind of awkwardly, considering.

Outside it's raining, the wet streets an empty urban slick. I get on my bike, cycle home, past the remnants of the Berlin Wall now covered in street art for the tourists, and the Oberbaumbrücke, the extravagantly turreted gothic bridge that straddles the Spree. All that night and for a long time afterwards, my head is full of echoes, flashes of light and colour, touch, and the persistent rhythm of the machines, beeping like life support.

JOHN MCCULLOUGH

POETRY

CALCULI

Storms make me travel into myself. I lie in bed and notice things: how each fingernail is a screensaver of somewhere I've never been, a white hill beneath a giant sky of pink that's ghosted with cloud, a country my hands have dreamed.

I have given this body many names across the years – prophet, demon, twit. Once: palace of failures. *The mice behind the skirting sing like birds*, I thought, *but I can't hear them*. The sycamores, too, for all I knew. My body – what a vessel to be stuck in! What a gruesome vase that kept on dribbling through all its holes so I had to clean it every day until I died.

Then I found it harboured other cargo, stealthy freight concealed beneath my liver's right lobe. A crystalline accumulation – suspicions hardened into certainties. I woke at 3 am with an angular pain below my sternum, radiating to my shoulder. I phoned a taxi with one hand clutched to my useless, breaking torso. I thought of Carnea, Roman goddess of not just organs but door handles, how I'd grown one inside me and it was forcing me to open.

Surgeons expanded me with gas, used special forceps to coax out my secrets. I came to as someone rattled peppercorns inside a jar. *Enough there to build a house!*

Wounds made my body tight. My walking speed was close to zero miles per hour. This, however, is the stone of it: there was a door in the middle of the desert. I noticed things – snails sliding up walls, the shape of bricks, how a roof can talk with sky. How every stem and slab and footstep's a sinewed thought of a world that's always dreaming.

I do not need another vessel to better comprehend the dark. I am already part of it, already sending out white hills to join leaves falling, to bump along with tuneful mice singing through the night, with every pebble that begins among a family deep inside the public earth.

PELICAN

December nights, I hold anxiety in front of me, electric yellow, like a giant beak.
It smacks into things. The milk I splash in my tea becomes a jellyfish and that entails
being stung, that takes me to a neat image of death, an idea like a Weeping Angel,
far away then suddenly at my shoulder, enfolding me in its wings. I look up at stars
that aren't there, that raced off millennia ago, rushing as far away as they could.
On TV, there is a beluga whale that mimics human voices and the carrying of objects.
I, too, imitate but keep dropping the objects and screeching in avian fashion,
my throat pouch trembling, my mind always suspecting *Have you got a cigarette*
will lead to *Give me your wallet.*
                                        Then my beak smacks into something else.
I remember the Victorian zoologist who drew jellyfish on all his Christmas cards
like dazzling chandeliers. Festive tentacles. From my broken fairy light, a little genie
of smoke arises, my lover's voice on the phone. I'm not a bird at all but a man drawn
on folded wrapping paper – cut out and pulled into fifteen of myself by his *hello baby.*

MUMPSIMUS

'postman's knock ... has nothing to do with dead men at the door'
    Rebecca Perry, *Pow*

Someone left a dictionary on the wall outside my house:
a gift, a threat. The wind riffles through, flumps back,

unsure it has the right first letter. Leaving home, I'm snagged
by words – not meanings but the images they unfold.

Flap dragon, an angry letterbox. *X-ray slap*, make-up
that shows you're broken. I come to, streets away,

no memory of walking there. Lost language always seems
to lead to lost time, to endless trekking, fruitless searches.

If I could find the perfect word this would all be over.
It often seems so close I swear if I keep talking and talking

it will tumble out, the something on which it all depends.
I pause just to cool down, prevent combustion.

The dictionary's mislaid its spine and cover so, while shut,
might be mistaken for a block of ice. Each word's retrievable,

could lead to magic. The decline of the jellygraph
as a copying device and measurement of fear doesn't mean

we shouldn't say *jellygraph* at every given chance.
The dictionary lies open in thunderstorms, its sodden pages

catching syllables. *Coracle*, an underwater prophet.
Rum peeper, the reflection at the bottom of a glass.

I keep thinking of the leap month that appeared in certain
years in Rome, whether it might arrive again if its name

were spoken often enough, and warmly. *Mercedonius* . . .
Sun-dried, the dictionary's pages curl, begin to yellow.

Sad creature: no one wants its dreams. I stroke its binding
before I head inside and forget about it for a while,

this wounded animal I can't contain, that can't contain me.

REUNION

VERA GIACONI
tr. MEGAN MCDOWELL

I hadn't seen them in fifteen months, and in that time my life hadn't changed at all. I was still in the same apartment, still single, working as a freelance editor and copy-editor for the same publishers. I hadn't changed my haircut and I was almost sure I was wearing the same pair of sandals I'd had on the last time we had dinner together. I'd had two more or less stable relationships that had begun and ended without much enthusiasm. And one unmentionable night with a guy with a cleft lip.

They, on the other hand, had just returned after years spent living abroad in various cities, each more exotic than the last; I didn't even know where they'd been living most recently. For the past year and a half they'd barely communicated with me or anyone else, but they'd let me know they had lost a large part of their fortune (which was huge), and that they'd become the parents of a little girl named Mali.

'It worked,' Clara had told me over the phone when they finally called to let me know they had returned.

What exactly did it meant that it had 'worked'? What was it that had worked? While I was driving to Clara and Javier's house right in the middle of Belgrano, I kept thinking about what Clara had said to me and regretting that I'd done the same thing that I always did with her: behave as though the things she said were perfectly logical and understandable. But I hadn't understood. In general I understood little of what Clara told me in a confidential tone of voice. Clara had suffered several miscarriages, and the logical thing was that she meant she had finally been able to have a baby. But no one uses a word like 'worked' to give news like that, and I also couldn't believe that they'd waited until then to tell me. Nor could I understand why I had to follow all the instructions she'd given me before I could visit them. I hadn't asked questions. I never asked anything when Clara acted as if I was up to all of her insinuations. I really wanted to be up to them.

*

Clara and I had gone to high school together, but we didn't make friends until we moved to Buenos Aires to study and our parents, who *were* friends, decided to share expenses on the apartment on Agrelo we moved into.

In Neochea we'd had different groups of friends. I let my hair grow very long and wore canvas sneakers and listened to national rock. My friends and I smoked and talked back to the teachers and spent the whole school year dissecting the things we'd talked about with the boys from the capital we'd met the summer before. Clara, on the other hand, cut her blonde hair very short, trying to call as little attention to her beauty as possible, and she spent all her time alone; she never went to our class parties, and some kind of medical allowance kept her on the sidelines in all our school's sporting activities. Her only friend had committed suicide in our last year of high school. She'd hung herself from one of the trees in her backyard. For a while, we'd all looked at Clara as if we expected her to do the same. But Clara didn't kill herself. I never talked to her about that, not even years later.

I studied Communication, then Literature, then Publishing. I didn't get a degree in any of them. Clara majored in Economics, and that's where she met Javier. The distance between Clara and me, which not even our living together had managed to overcome entirely, disappeared as soon as Javier set foot in our apartment the first time. That night, we drank Baileys and smoked and talked until dawn. We were inseparable for the next four years.

I involved them in long sessions of film theory, the analysis of everything I was reading at university; I dragged them on bike rides in El Tigre, to the Ecological Reserve, to the Costanera, and I managed to convince them to spend our vacations camping in inhospitable locations during the off-season. Clara, in turn, carted us from spiritualist sessions to some awkward attempts at yoga and meditation, and she subjected us to her experiments in vegetarian food. Javier took it upon himself to introduce us to acid and electronic music. The apartment gradually turned into a cross-section of all our phases and whims, and Javier's ever more sophisticated computers coexisted happily alongside Clara's scented candles and Tarot cards, and my books that at some point I began to pile up directly on the floor.

Sometimes I think that with them I wasted my chance to be part of a real couple. No relationship seemed as fun or as challenging as the time the three of us spent together.

Of course, at some point I fell in love with Javier. Or I made a great effort not to fall in love with him. Or I fell in love with the idea of being part of the couple in our trio and not the extra piece. I never talked about this with either of them; I knew it could ruin everything. And they did their part to make things easy for me. Clara's room and mine were separated by a wall so thin it was basically just a sheet of drywall, but the nights Javier slept over – which was almost always – I never heard anything that happened between them once they were on their own. And I don't mean that I didn't hear them screw or laugh or talk. I mean they didn't make a sound. As if once they went through the door into Clara's room, they just disappeared. Nor did they kiss in my presence, or make any private jokes.

At times I liked to think that without me, they were also lost, as if I were the best reason they had to be together. But then Javier graduated and got a job at a Brazilian mega-corporation, and in less than three months they got married and went to live in São Paulo. Later there would be other destinations – Barcelona, London, Shanghai – but at that moment, when the news about São Paulo came, I was despondent. Reproaching them or letting them see my despair put me in a position I didn't like at all, a dark place full of resentment and envy. What I did, then, was hug them, propose a toast to all the good news, and participate in all the preparations for the wedding and the move.

*

For two years, I was the only person they stayed in touch with. Clara's mother called me to get news about her daughter. Now, from a distance, I feel that what I told her during those conversations (they're fine, healthy, progressing) were lies. But no, it was all true, it was just that those truths didn't even touch on the most meaningful part of Clara and Javier's life in São Paulo, in particular the two events that would mark the beginning of everything that would happen to them later: they killed a man in a car accident, and, not long after, Clara lost a baby eight months along.

According to Clara, the accident and the miscarriage were entirely related. They'd gone to a party at the embassy. Javier had had a lot to drink and Clara was even worse, which was why she didn't insist they go home in a taxi. It was a bright night, and the avenue was deserted. Both of them swear the guy came out of nowhere, as if he had thrown himself onto the car on purpose. After hitting him at full speed and seeing the body fly over the windshield, Javier lost control of the car and it turned over. When the ambulance arrived, the guy was already dead. Clara and Javier were unharmed, but they spent a night in the hospital under observation. Clara couldn't sleep, and early in the morning she got up to wander the hallways. They hadn't been taken to the private clinic their insurance paid for, but rather to a public hospital. And while she was wandering, Clara encountered the widow. She saw her in the entrance to intensive care. Somehow, they recognised each other. The woman, short and dark, had six children with her. The youngest was maybe three, and the oldest no more than fifteen. Clara thought about going over to say something; she wanted to cry, apologise, explain, but the woman's eyes dissuaded her. She saw the woman ask a nurse a question. The nurse looked at Clara, then at the newly widowed woman, and murmured an answer. The widow took two steps toward where Clara stood, looking her directly in the eyes. Then she spat on her left hand, rubbed her belly with it and shouted something unintelligible. Clara hurried back to her room and didn't sleep for the rest of the night. The doctor discharged them at eight in the morning, and she got dressed to go and meet Javier at reception. When she emerged from the room, she saw that on the floor just outside the door, there was a clay plate with seven fish heads on it. Just then, the lawyer the company had sent for them arrived. He was a sweaty man around 50 years old, and he squeezed Clara's arm with a damp hand while he told her not to worry, that he would take care of everything. When he said 'everything', Clara stole a glance at the plate full of fish heads, and the lawyer winked at her.

Clara got pregnant a few months after the accident, and they didn't tell anyone anything, except me. According to Javier, Clara never left the apartment, and she wouldn't allow visitors. She was convinced that if news of the pregnancy reached the ears of anyone linked to the guy they had killed, they would take her baby as payback, harvest her baby not as revenge, but as retribution.

Clara constantly recalled the widow rubbing her own belly, and she knew it had been a curse. Javier told her the gesture could mean anything.

They each dealt with the situation in their own way. During those days, Clara started to practice certain magical rituals. She did it on her own, reading a lot and improvising a bit. Sometimes what she was after was to protect herself; other times, to make offerings. But most of her ceremonies were variations on the same theme: asking forgiveness. And Javier, although the courts had acquitted them of any crime or guilt, had gone to great lengths to falsify a few papers for the deceased man. They designed a life insurance policy and a special pension from who knows where, and in that way they made sure the widow and her kids would receive a sum of money that they would never have even dreamed of before. 'We're paying dearly,' Javier told Clara.

One afternoon, Clara sat on the bed for hours, motionless, with both hands over her belly: she couldn't feel the baby, no movement, nothing. When Javier came back from work, late that night, Clara told him the baby was dead. The ride to the clinic was endless and silent until Clara seemed to wake up. She reached over to caress Javier's neck, and said, 'Now we're really starting to pay.' A few hours later, when Clara had fallen asleep, Javier stepped outside and called me. Right away I could tell he wasn't sad but rather worried, or anxious.

'Is she all right?' I asked.

'The doctors say she'll be fine, that it's more normal than people think for these things to happen.'

'And you? How are you?'

'It bothers me that she said "starting",' he said, 'that we've just *started* to pay.'

*

Not long after that, Javier was promoted again and they moved to Barcelona. Once again it was Javier who called to tell me, and I told him that starting over again in a new place was the best thing that could happen to them. Javier begged me to come and visit.

I let him buy me a ticket and pay for my stay (with what I earned I wouldn't have been able to cover even half of those expenses), but when I got to Barcelona I settled into a cheap hostel that I'd chosen myself. Clara and I talked on the phone every day, but she didn't let me visit her until later. She said she still wasn't ready to see anyone. I knew her, and I knew that if I insisted it would only make things worse. So I sat in a booth at the internet cafe next door, and we had long conversations while I watched the boys and girls staying at the hostel as they came and went. They all looked so young to me. A bit awkward, and uninhibited. Watching them spill through the streets with so much energy made me feel old, or more like worn out, although between them and me there couldn't have been more than six or seven years difference. Maybe it was the influence of Clara, who during that time had developed the voice of an old woman, and talked as if she were a hundred years old. She started her sentences by clearing her throat and ended them whispering, as if speaking left her exhausted. In one of those conversations, Clara told me: 'It was a huge relief.' We'd been talking about the ceremony that she and Javier had organised to say farewell to their unborn daughter, in a beautiful private cemetery on the outskirts of São Paulo.

Javier was grateful for my patience; he was sure that at some point Clara would agree to see me and that I would help her, that I was the only one who could help her. To me, all those days of waiting started to seem a bit ridiculous, but I didn't say anything. Javier didn't need any more pressure. I saw him almost every night; he took me to eat at his favourite places and tried to act natural. But without Clara, our meetings were slightly uncomfortable.

One week after I arrived, Clara finally agreed to let me come and see her. She was the one who opened the door to the imposing apartment the company had rented for them, and she gave me a long hug. She had grown much thinner, and was too pale.

'I was starting to think you only existed in my imagination,' she said.

Clara's clothes, and Javier's, and the walls of the apartment, the rugs, the furniture, everything seemed like a giant cross-section of beige and white shades. With my red sneakers, jean skirt, and striped green shirt, I felt phosphorescent, and not in a good way. Still, neither of them seemed to notice.

That time, my presence had the same effect as Javier's first visit to our apartment on Agrelo. All the distances disappeared and it wasn't long before we felt like the old days again, when everything was easy, safe, and stimulating. We didn't talk about anything important, or mention the accident or the pregnancy. We simply let the time pass as we recalled anecdotes and old conversations. We ended up all three of us barefoot, sitting on the floor around the coffee table, eating some last-minute pizzas straight from the box with our hands, and drinking, without paying the slightest attention, one bottle after another of expensive wine from the cellar Javier had started to keep.

'You all are some truly hoity-toity snobs,' I told them, and I felt the air move too fast around me.

'Hoity-toity snobs!' Javier repeated with an abrupt gesture, laughing and jabbing his index finger in the air. The cherry from the joint he'd just rolled fell onto the rug and burned a hole.

I tried to put it out but I only made it worse, and the hole turned into a large black stain. For some reason this struck Clara as very interesting, and she crawled over to Javier. I had to climb up onto the sofa to let her past, and from there I watched as she took the joint from Javier, lit it again, took a drag, and used the lit end to make another hole in the rug. Javier imitated her. They made at least five more holes, until there was nothing left to burn it with. Then Clara got my cigarettes out of my backpack. Although I detest white in all its forms, beige in particular, I just couldn't convince myself it was a good idea to burn such a fine carpet, and much less to risk torching the whole apartment. But

I let them do it because there was something fascinating in the way they went around on all fours, crawling over the rug that covered much of the living room floor, just so they could dot it with big black holes. It was fascinating and a little disturbing, because it was the first private accord between Clara and Javier that I had witnessed, the first time they'd left me completely out, and as such it was the first time I could see them from a certain distance. They struck me as powerful. I stayed on one of the sofas, with my legs crossed and without touching the floor so as to leave them room. When they finished the last cigarette, they looked each other in the eyes and then they noticed me, as if I'd been hiding and had just caught them by surprise.

'Hi, reality,' Clara said to me then, and they both started to laugh.

I stayed for over fifteen days, and in that time Clara returned completely to the world. That led me to meet many of the new people who quickly started to form part of Clara's and Javier's social life (and who I tried to avoid): his colleagues, the wives of his colleagues, and a German teacher and her judge husband, who were neighbours of Clara and Javier and who for some reason fitted in perfectly with the rest of the group. Everyone fitted in except for me. I went back to Barcelona a couple more times, always at the request of one of them and paid for by them, until Javier was promoted again and they sent him to London. In all the months they lived in that apartment, they never replaced the rug.

'I feel like we go farther away every time,' said Clara.

I had to stay strong during the storm of proposals with which they tried to shorten a distance that they were starting to feel as almost definitive. The first thing was to convince them that it wasn't a good idea for me to move with them to London. I told a few lies, like that things were starting to go well for me at work, when really what I thought was that the last thing I needed was for them to drag me from one destination to another as if I were the family poodle. The second was to very carefully turn down the offer to work as their representative and to take care of all of Clara and Javier's matters and investments in Buenos Aires. I didn't want to be their employee, either. The only thing I agreed to was for Javier to buy the apartment on Agrelo and to put it in my name. It was a real relief to get out from under the rent. By then I was doing correction work for several publishers, and my parents were still sending me a little money every month, but I never had enough to stop worrying. Clara was pleased with the agreement. I think that, deep down, she thought that the apartment would go on belonging to them a little, and that way I would be a dot on the map, marking the place where one day they would have to return.

*

Javier went on climbing the ladder at the company, and from London they transferred him to Shanghai. After a few years he succumbed to the overtures of another company and an even better job, and they left Shanghai, but I never knew where they went. I never understood what exactly Javier did (I knew it had something to do with the stock market, finance, and things like that), and he never really made much effort to explain it to me. Really, it was more like he avoided the subject. Not as though he felt ashamed or was being discreet, but as though he found it all terribly boring. 'It's just a way to make money,' he'd say.

A lot of money, I thought.

If Clara and Javier's time in São Paulo had been turbulent, the years in London, and especially in Shanghai, were frenetic. It was as if all the activity, the things they tried, the people who joined their lives for brief and euphoric periods, were a way of exorcising all the rest. Because Clara got pregnant again in London, and again she lost the baby. After the third spontaneous abortion, though they announced each pregnancy to me with all their hopes intact, I could only wonder how long it would last this time, and the wait became nerve-wracking. I stood by for every bit of news from them, and they made sure to keep me in the loop, and always included me in whatever they were doing when I went to stay with them for a few weeks in one of their new cities. By chance, or because they made sure of it (I never asked), my visits never coincided with any of the pregnancies. I was always with them for what came after, which was the intense search for excitement that would give them the break they needed to get their strength back and start over. There was also magic. Clara was more and more caught up in a series of rites and magical diagrams with which she explained everything that happened to them, and that she used to justify all the important decisions of their lives. She said that she'd had several teachers (I hadn't met any of them), but that she was learning the most important part on her own. We didn't talk much about that because Clara quickly realised that I wasn't convinced, and, according to her, my distrust could work against her. Beyond my scepticism, the truth is that the whole thing scared me a little. I had the feeling that those two, Clara and magic, were forces that shouldn't be crossed, at least not without a mediator who could direct them, or control them.

In all those years, the only place I never visited was the last city they lived in. During the fifteen months they spent there, they never invited me to visit, and their few emails spoke only of their 'new home'. From the start it had been impossible to get them on the phone, and it took them months to reply to an email. The last I'd heard before a long silence was that Clara was pregnant again. Her eighth pregnancy, no less. Every once in a while I'd receive a very impersonal message, the bare minimum to avoid cutting off contact for good, and I got a present from them for my most recent birthday: a bottle of perfume. The box and the bottle (a drop of crystal covered with fine nerves of pure gold) were enough for me to know that it was very, very expensive. And yet, I found it unbearable. At first it was a citric scent, intense and pleasant, but it wouldn't come off with water or alcohol, and as the hours passed it transformed until it reminded me of the smell of a wet dog. In other times I would have made a joke about their terrible choice, but at that point I felt I couldn't make a comment like that, maybe bordering on offensive. And that led me to realise that in all that time, not only had they known how to administer their silences so as not to wound me or give me reason to complain, but also that something fundamental had ceased to exist between us, as if they had finally found the way to be alone, the two of them, in good times and in bad, like Clara used to say about the three of us.

Every time I thought about how long it had been since I'd heard anything from them, I also thought about how I still hadn't received the call from Javier (he was always the one who called) to let me know that Clara had lost her latest pregnancy. I held on to that idea to strengthen my theory that they had finally done it, that they were parents at last, and that was why they didn't have room in their lives for anyone else, not even me. That was, definitely, the only explanation for our growing apart that was less painful for me, even though it meant that for some reason they'd decided not to share the big news with me.

I found out about Mali only once they were back in Buenos Aires, the afternoon Clara called to tell me that they'd arrived, that they wanted to see me, that Javier had resigned from the company so they could settle definitively here, and that they'd expect me for dinner the following Saturday. She also told me to wear the perfume they'd sent me, and to bring something for Mali. The instructions about the perfume and the gift weren't things that Clara mentioned in passing. She made sure to moderate her voice and to pause before and after she said them so I would understand that they were very clear specifications, almost conditions, as if seeing them depended on my compliance with those rules. Finally, she made me swear that I wouldn't tell anyone, absolutely anyone, that they'd returned.

*

I parked my car outside Clara and Javier's house. Under my arm I was carrying the big package with the gift for Mali (a stuffed cow that said 'mooooo' when you squeezed its nose and that, just then, struck me as a stupid choice). I was also wearing the perfume, and though I still smelled like oranges and plums, I knew that soon I would stink of wet dog.

The gate was open, and as I walked along the path to the door I tried to catch a glimpse of Clara and Javier's silhouettes in the front windows. The whole house was lit up. I rang the doorbell and felt an emptiness in the pit of my stomach, like a slight nausea.

'Did you bring the present?' It was Clara's voice. She was talking to me through the closed door.

I told her I had, speaking toward the darkness of the peephole.

'What is it?'

'A stuffed animal. A cow.' I was about to laugh. I wanted to think that Clara was in the middle of one of her games.

'And the perfume?'

'I'm all bathed and perfumed,' I replied.

Clara opened the door a crack and she seemed to sniff the air, or me, really, as if she were her own guard dog.

'Are you OK?' I asked her then, as she opened the door just enough to let me in.

'Yes,' she replied, and it was true.

Clara looked incredibly beautiful, but in a disturbing way, because she reminded me of the teenager I had known before all the travelling, before the accident, before the dead babies, even before Javier. Her blonde hair was again cut very short, and she was wearing a long white dress that also covered her arms and the base of her neck, even though outside, and also in the house, it was hot. She was so beautiful it was uncomfortable to look at her, because it was like standing before something manufactured and corrected to perfection, like an animation or a hologram. I lingered on the thought that beauty treatments, when a person has time and money, sure can work wonders.

I took a few steps toward her as though to hug or kiss her, but Clara moved fast: she took the present from my hands and stepped back, then darted around me to close the door behind me. And then I could get a look at Mali. She'd been hidden behind Clara.

She was a little girl, not a baby, a child who looked to be around six years old. How was it possible that this was Clara and Javier's daughter? Then I told myself that they had adopted, that Clara had finally decided to consider other options. I tried to meet Clara's eyes, expecting her to say something, but Clara wasn't looking at me. Her eyes were fixed on the little girl, and she was smiling with an expression that was a mixture of relief and tenderness. Mali had long, straight black hair, and her dark eyes shone. She was wearing a pink cotton dress and some impeccable white shoes, but under her clothes she was dirty: I saw streaks of dirt on her arms and neck, and her nails were long and grimy.

Clara said my name and Mali's to introduce us. And the little girl smiled. It was as chilling as if I'd seen a cat smile. She said something in a language I didn't recognise, a closed and guttural language that made me think she wasn't speaking, but grunting. Everything about her reminded me of a little wild animal.

'She wants you to hug her,' Clara translated.

Mali had reached out her arms and she kept that smile on her face. I knelt down so I'd be at her level and I let the girl wrap her little arms around me. She held on tightly while she buried her nose against my neck and in my hair. She was sniffing me, the way Clara had. When she finally let go of me, the girl wasn't smiling any more, she was making a sort of snorting sound, and when she looked at Clara I couldn't tell if her expression was disappointment or anger. I took a step back and Clara grabbed my arm tightly.

'You'll be OK,' she told me. Her voice sounded as young as she looked. Then she hugged me and looked me in the eyes: 'We missed you so much.' And at last I could see something of Clara in Clara.

She led me to the eat-in kitchen. I had never been in that house, but I recognised Clara's taste in the leather armchairs and the curtains of very fine, un-patterned fabric, in the natural wooden mouldings and floors, in the lit candles placed strategically around to make everything look warm and homely. But there was something different. Outside, the air smelled like summer, jasmine, dampness and fire. Inside it smelled like wet paper, steam, rotten milk and hard-boiled eggs. I discreetly covered my nose.

When we got to the kitchen, Mali was already there; she was squatting on the table. Javier had his back to us as he kept watch over several pots that were boiling simultaneously on the stove.

'Javi,' said Clara, to get his attention.

Javier turned and looked at me with an enormous smile. He looked younger, too. With two agile steps he was beside me, hugging me tightly and saying:

'I'm so happy, so happy...' His voice sounded so sincere that I couldn't help it, I returned his hug in silence.

Over Javier's arm, I could see Clara as she handed the package with my gift to Mali, who tore it open in two fast motions. She held the big stuffed cow level with her eyes, looked at it curiously, and brought her face close to the cow's, maybe to smell it the way she'd done with me. She pressed the cow's snout with her nose and it let out a loud 'mooooo'. The girl gave a shrill cry and dropped the cow in fright.

I started, but Clara and Javier were stiff, looking at her as if they were afraid the girl was going to explode or spontaneously burst into flames. But Mali turned her head to look at me, then she looked at the inoffensive stuffed animal lying on the floor, and she started to laugh. Her peals of laughter were agonising, a sound more like a kid having an asthma attack than one who was happy. Clara and Javier started breathing again.

Then one of the pots started boiling over and Javier ran to turn off the flame. He started taking hard boiled eggs from the pot and holding them under cold water from the faucet to cool them. He took out over a dozen. Clara had picked up the stuffed cow and she whispered a question into Mali's ear, which the girl responded to by nodding yes.

'She's very grateful, really,' said Clara, hugging the animal. 'I'm going to put it away and I'll be right back.'

She turned around and was gone, leaving me alone with Javier, who never stopped looking at me and smiling, and with the little girl, who started to gobble down the hardboiled eggs that Javier began to peel and hand to her.

'Are you guys OK?' I asked, mostly to break the uncomfortable silence.

'Something like that,' he said. 'We're getting used to things.'

And there it was, a typical phrase of Clara's coming from Javier's mouth. They, who had always managed to be two individuals in spite of all the years they'd spent together, were starting to speak the same. But with him I wasn't going to fall into the trap of acting as if I'd understood what he was trying to say.

'Getting used to what?' I asked him, and with his head he indicated Mali, who, ignoring us, was still squatting on top of the table and eating the eggs as if they were ears of corn, holding them with both hands and taking small, quick bites.

'Your turn,' he said to me then, I guess to change the subject, and he handed me a little jar filled with milk that had been on the lit stove.

'She'll burn herself.'

'It's good like that.'

I used a dishcloth as a potholder, took the jar, and set it on the table a few centimetres from Mali. The girl left an egg half-eaten and pounced on the milk, drinking it straight from the jar in long gulps.

'Javier, what is this?' I asked, indicating the girl.

He looked me in the eyes and I realised he was confused, as if he really didn't understand what I was talking about.

Just then, Clara came into the kitchen.

'*This* is my daughter,' she told me in a severe voice.

Javier looked at her as though in apology. But she passed quickly between us and picked up Mali, who obediently let herself be lifted.

'I'm going to take her to her room.'

Mali looked at me over Clara's shoulder and stuck out her tongue.

'You have to understand her,' said Javier.

He cleaned the remains of egg from the table, put the little milk jug in the refrigerator and opened a bottle of wine. I sat down across from him, trying to seem calm even as I was aware that this was the moment to clear things up. When he was alone, Javier was more frank, or more vulnerable.

'We have a lot to talk about,' I told him as he handed me a glass.

'We've never gone so long without seeing each other, have we?'

'Over a year,' I said.

'Yes,' said Javier as he poured wine into our glasses. 'Over a year.'

'I don't know anything about the last place you lived,' I told him, to test the ground. 'I never heard anything from you two in all that time. I didn't even know about Mali until a few days ago...'

Javier looked at me over the rim of his glass, surprised.

'But Clara told me you knew everything. She wrote to you all the time,' he said.

I shook my head.

'Then, you don't know anything?'

'Nothing.'

'Then what are you doing here?' he asked, standing up suddenly as if he'd been caught doing something wrong.

'Clara called me when you got here, a few days ago, and she invited me over.'

'When did she call?'

'Monday, I think...'

'This Monday?'

I said yes, and he started darting around nervously, glancing past me as though looking for Clara before saying anything else, and as if I, suddenly, had become a person who could cause him harm. The burners were still on and the milk in one of the pots boiled over and put out the flame. The kitchen started to smell like gas. Javier reacted like a clumsy teenager, and instead of turning off the gas and opening a window, he first worried about getting the pot off the stove. He burned himself on the handle, dropped the pot, and spilled the boiling milk all over the floor. Then he wanted to take care of the spilled milk, while the gas went on filling the air. I leapt up to help him but he shouted, 'I've got it!'

And then, finally, he managed to put things in the correct order. He left the cloth on the floor, turned off the gas, and opened the kitchen windows wide. The air cooled quickly and I took a deep breath.

Then he was back on his knees on the floor, cleaning up the milk with a rag. He only made it worse, but he kept doing it; it was clear he would rather do anything than talk to me. At that moment Clara came back, saw what had happened and knelt down next to Javier. He burst into tears as soon as she was beside him and Clara hugged him, caressing his hair while she soothed him. I felt like an intruder. Someone incapable of understanding what she was seeing and thus not worthy of being a witness. Javier was crying disconsolately, and Clara acted as if it weren't the first time he'd behaved that way. There was something mechanical in her consoling gestures. As if it was no longer necessary to focus on what she was doing or pay attention to what was happening in order to know how to act and when to stop.

'Easy now. She has the perfume, did you smell it?' she asked, indicating me with her eyes. 'And it worked, didn't it? She's safe. We would have realised if it wasn't working,' she added, and she winked at him, as if she'd just cracked a joke.

'Safe from what...' I tried to interrupt.

But Clara and Javier were out of my reach.

'I didn't tell her anything because she wouldn't understand,' Clara went on. 'And I didn't tell you anything because I know how you worry about them.' Javier's sobs started to sound more like isolated hiccups; his breathing was agitated but there were no more tears, and Clara relaxed her arms a bit. 'You're worried about them both, aren't you?' Clara stretched one of her sleeves to dry the last of his tears. 'It's all OK.'

'But, what if she can't?' asked Javier.

Clara smiled tenderly.

'She'll be able to.'

All that time, I'd been motionless in my chair and watching them, just like the time they'd burned holes in the living room rug. And, also like that time, they soon came back from where they'd been and looked at me as if they'd just discovered me.

'Sorry,' I said. But I didn't know what I was apologising for.

Clara waved her hand as if to say I shouldn't worry, and Javier wiped his face with the same dirty rag he'd been cleaning the floor with. His face became a milky, dirty mask. Clara kissed his forehead and asked if he felt better. Javier nodded sheepishly and got to his feet, then took her by the hands and helped her up.

With Javier calmer now, Clara seemed to find the moment to turn to me, and she invited me to follow her. We walked silently to the living room, Clara in front, leading Javier by the hand, and me a few steps behind, in silence. By that point I couldn't even think of any question that would help me understand what I had seen since I entered that house.

'Sit down,' Clara told me as she settled into the big leather armchair.

I sat across from her, in a little chair that was sticky and smelled of damp. Javier sat on the floor, his legs crossed, staring at me.

'You know everything, I don't have to start from the beginning. And the important thing, in any case, is that you understand that we wanted this, that we're happy. Right, Javi?' Javier nodded yes. 'Maybe we should have asked for help, but we wanted to do it ourselves. We didn't know if anyone else would be willing to go to the the end...'

'The end of what?'

'Everything has an edge,' said Clara, leaning a little toward me, as if what she was about to say would start to form part of a secret. 'We paid and it wasn't fair to keep accepting it. And we decided enough was enough. Seven children. Seven. I wasn't willing to give even one more, understand?'

'Mali...'

'There were many ways we brought Mali into the world,' said Clara. 'And in each of those ways, Mali is our daughter. Ours.'

'But you can't do that.'

'It's a little more complicated than that,' said Clara.

Those are the last words I remember, because after that moment nothing really made sense. Suddenly it was like I had two Claras before me, one who was trying to tell me exactly what had happened, what they had done, and another who was doing everything possible to distract her from her goal. Javier didn't take his eyes off me. At no point did I try to interrupt her. For one thing, I thought that if I stayed quiet maybe she would forget she was talking to me and finally say something concrete, and for another I found the curves and digressions of her speech fascinating. Until I started to feel weakened, as if they'd hypnotised me. I felt like my hands were heavy, and so were my legs and eyelids, and a white spot appeared and disappeared in front of my eyes. At the same time, the nausea had passed and suddenly I started to feel hungry, very hungry.

Clara paused and I took the chance to ask them for something to eat.

'You're hungry?' Clara asked.

I said yes and they both started to laugh. They seemed truly relieved. Two relieved and happy lunatics.

'Excellent!' cried Clara. 'That's excellent.'

She signalled to Javier and he ran off to the kitchen. For a second I worried that for those two, dinner meant a bunch of hardboiled eggs and a glass of milk. But it was worse. Javier appeared with an enormous silver tray, one that they used to use in the magnificent parties they'd given back when they had been themselves. It held three glasses of wine already poured and a porcelain dish with big pieces of nearly raw meat, wrapped in some dark leaves that looked like seaweed. It was like a crazy, carnivorous version of sushi. Javier set the tray on the coffee table and Clara distributed the glasses and proposed a toast.

'To Mali,' she said.

At that point I was only thinking about leaving, getting out of that house and leaving them behind so I could be alone and cry for my friends. Clara offered me one of the chunks of meat. Although I would have preferred not to touch the stuff, they both sat looking at me and I felt I had no choice. Plus, if that was the price I had to pay to get out of there, I was willing to endure it. I put the morsel in my mouth and started to chew. The meat oozed blood and the green stuff (which wasn't seaweed) gave off a bitter juice that made my eyes fill with tears. The nausea returned.

'Swallow,' Clara said impatiently.

I took a long sip of wine (which had turned to vinegar) and forced myself to swallow it all in spite of my gagging. Clara and Javier smiled again, they clapped, even, and I thought 'enough'. I wanted to stand but I was weak; I felt my heart pound and my back break out in sweat, as if I were about to faint. My vision grew blurry but I could make out Clara's face, she'd come to stand in front of me and was caressing my forehead.

'See?' I heard her say to Javier. 'It's over, she's out...'

*

I don't know how long I was unconscious. When I woke up I was alone. They'd laid me on the sofa and covered me with a blanket. I had a bad headache, and my mouth, throat, and stomach were burning. By my feet I saw they'd left my backpack, which held my wallet and car keys, even though when I'd arrived, Clara had whisked it away somewhere. I called to Clara, to Javier, but no one answered. The ground floor was in silence, but I heard voices coming from the second floor. The house was now in shadows. Only the kitchen light had been left on, and it barely illuminated anything in the living room; the street light filtered in between the curtains. I looked at the clock. Three in the morning. I stood up slowly – I was very dizzy – and walked to the foot of the stairs.

'Clara!' I cried. 'Clara! Javier!' I shouted louder.

I breathed deeply and started up the stairs, feeling my way on each step. Everything on the upper floor was also in darkness, except for a faint light that blinked in one of the last rooms. I walked silently down the hallway I peered into the last room and there they were: Clara, Javier, and Mali, sitting on the floor. At the back of the room was a big basket woven from bamboo, and the floor was covered with a thick green rug that reminded me of artificial grass.

Mali was crouched down, grasping one of Clara's small breasts with both hands, with her teeth clamped into the flesh. She was sucking hard. Clara looked up at me and smiled sweetly, as if I'd just walked in on her nursing a newborn. She was caressing Javier's hair; his head was resting on her lap and he was sleeping with the relaxed face and serene breathing of a child.

There was something about the light, the way it fell on the faces of the three of them, that made me leave aside my fear and disgust, and managed to move me a bit. They were the same. The three of them. Or versions of the same being.

Clara stopped caressing Javier and reached out a hand to summon me closer. I was shaking. I walked slowly until I was beside her. Mali glanced up at me, but Clara murmured something to her and she went back to what she was doing.

'I love you,' Clara told me in a whisper, 'but you have to leave.'

'What did you do?' I asked, although the answers didn't matter so much to me any more. I would have liked to drag her out of there with me, or to put my head in her lap, too, and cry.

'I'm sorry for making you come here, but I needed you to meet her, to see me. I'm sorry for everything, but rest assured that I was careful and that you're going to be all right. She's not going to follow you, and we're not either. This doesn't have anything to do with anyone, we didn't do it against anyone. I want you to know that.'

For a second I tried to think of something else to say to her, but right away I felt that the best thing to do was what I had always done with her: act as if I'd understood everything.

'You can't talk about this to anyone, or tell anyone we came back. And you can't ever come here again,' she told me.

Mali looked at me again, fixedly. Without ceasing her suctioning she started to wrinkle her nose as if she were sniffing me again, as if she'd forgotten that we'd already been through this and she was starting everything all over again. Clara saw her and told me: 'Get going.'

And when I didn't react, she shouted:

'Now!'

KERSTIN BRÄTSCH   INTERVIEW

It's beside the point to consider any single painting by Kerstin Brätsch; her pieces accumulate in power like tomograms taken from a wider, ecstatic, outward-reaching project. Her signature works – oil paintings on large sheets of transparent Mylar or paper – harness a heady amalgam of the lacy striations of agate, the swampy figuration of Jean Dubuffet, the twists of radiated entrails, the striding black gestures of Robert Motherwell, and Jersey Shore airbrushing. But while her style is distinctive, Brätsch's forms and methods are diverse. The Hamburg-born, New York-based artist, who was the recipient of the Edvard Munch Art Award 2017, returns to the embryonic elements of painting – pigment, oil, and light; the artist's hand and the movement required to constitute a gesture – subjecting each to various operations of distillation, chance, outsourcing, and layering. Her aim, it would seem, is to coax from painting what might still be unknown.

For this reason, it's not immediately apparent why Brätsch's work should so often warrant inclusion in exhibitions that tackle the now old-chestnut dilemma of painting's status in 'the digital era'. She was, for example, included in Museum Brandhorst's sweeping *Painting 2.0: Expression in the information age* (2015), MoMA's *The Forever Now* (2014), and the Fridericianum's *Speculations on Anonymous Materials* (2014). Her reckoning with the impact of the digital on visual culture – its networks and atemporality, its conduciveness to sampling and versioning and editing, and the ubiquitous frame of the screen – is explicitly material. Though her paintings translate lusciously to a screen, they also double-down on every ineffable and substantial thing that evades reduction to a pixel. Notwithstanding the modern techniques available to her, she turns continually to ancient technologies of marbling and glasswork. She turns to the earth, and to spirits, and to the people surrounding her.

During our conversation, Brätsch referenced octopi at least twice. A central tenet of her praxis is collaboration – the more hands on a project, the better. She works with artists, artisans, and with psychics and shamans (her 2006-08 series *Psychic* consists of abstract portraits she painted after meeting with clairvoyants in New York). These partnerships allow her to experiment with painting in a social context, considering its circulation, its relationship to sculpture, or identity, or marketing. They also question the nature of authorship, by foregrounding the community that always participates in the knowledge and production that ultimately constitute an artwork. As the text that appears in a painting as part of the installation *Sigis Erben* (2012) reads: 'DID I DO IT MYSELF? / IF SO – HELP ME / IF NOT – JOIN ME.'

After our conversation, I found a line from Dubuffet that applies as well to Brätsch's work as it does to our exchange: 'Art does not just lie in the bed we made for it; it would sooner run away than say its own name: what it likes is to be incognito. Its best moments are when it forgets what its own name is.'   ANNIE GODFREY LARMON

TWR   Across your collaborations and solo pursuits, it seems important to you to complicate hierarchies and authorship, and to employ horizontal models of making. Do you consider this mode of production to be a feminist one?

KB   There are definitely strands of feminist thinking present in how I create my work and live my life, but I am hesitant to call it feminist in this moment, because I feel like the word is used so flippantly in the media today. I also want to acknowledge that feminism is a constantly changing set of ideas, and I don't know if I have examined what it means today enough to apply it to my situation.

I believe in communities, and in that old word 'collaboration'. I believe that if I learn something, I also need to give my knowledge, pass it along. When I began working with artisans, for example, I wanted to put myself in Neophyte-like situations where I would have to observe and learn, about marbling, or glass, or stucco. During each of these experiences there has been a magical shift, where both of us, artist and craftsman, no longer know who we are. We swap identities, become a third. Two hands of a craftsman and two of an artist – we become a four-armed monster. Everything we know and are comfortable with is mixed and questioned. This is idealistic, but I believe moments like these provide a new perspective on familiar situations.

TWR   You started DAS INSTITUT with Adele Röder in 2007, and KAYA with Debo Eilers in 2010. How do these collaborations function? Do you consider these projects to be a destabilisation of the market-happy modernist 'genius'?

KB   I come from Germany, where it's impossible to avoid the notion of the lone male genius. When I was studying, there came a moment when I had to question this history and my understanding of it. I liked the idea of highlighting the relational aspect of painting, and there were many ways to do this: by playing with authorship, using painting as backdrop, or never showing a painting alone.

DAS INSTITUT started as a long-term conversation between Adele and me when we were students, and had an idealistic desire to create a structure that was bigger than ourselves. We wanted to invent a fictitious space, where we could exist as ourselves, but also experiment with each other's approaches. DAS INSTITUT is concerned with transfusing each other's ways of working and thinking, and with the possibility of trans-subjective activity. Ä becomes Ö, and we become Räder and Brötsch. We wanted to have tentacles, to reach outside, where other entities and identities could exist as well.

TWR   Does KAYA have a similar ethos?

KB   With KAYA, my collaborator Debo Eilers and I wanted to introduce a third entity into our work, a figure who would bring an unknown quality that we could react against. This led us to invite a 13-year-old named Kaya Serene to perform with us at the opening of our show at 179 Canal, NYC in 2010. We built a stage and invited Kaya to perform on it, giving her one of Debo's sculptures

to play with as she pleased – to add layers to, to deconstruct, to create something new. While this was happening, Debo was hiding from the audience underneath the stage creating paintings that were then passed on to me, to sign with my name. The paintings were then auctioned off by Margaret Lee who ran 179 Canal, a nonprofit artist-run space, to help her pay rent. We were interested in what it would mean for a sculptor to make paintings that would then be christened and signed by me, an actual painter, all thrown into relief by the presence and authorship of a 13-year-old girl.

Kaya is actually the daughter of a friend, and Debo and I stole her name for our collaboration. At the beginning Kaya was much more present in the process. She was a teenager, and we allowed her to intervene in the project and collaborate with us as she wished, inviting her to play with my name, lending her its cultural capital as a way to question hierarchies. It got to a point where we had to allow Kaya to mature, which meant being more mature in our relationship with her, disposing of our fascination with her age and acting our own age.

TWR   Perhaps you're bringing something impure to the hallowed grounds of painting – incorporating other practices into the field of solo work. Do you experience different pressures when you are working alone versus collectively?
KB   I am not sure if I make a distinction between the two, because there are different pressures even when working collectively as DAS INSTITUT and KAYA. My collaboration with Adele is based

upon a relationship between two German women. Debo is an American man, and so we deal with very different identities, hierarchies, and power structures. While DAS INSTITUT is much more ephemeral, KAYA is harsh and brutal. This dynamic reflects back onto the work – like our 'body bag' series, which I like to think of as DIY plastic surgery on 'painting bodies'. We start with a mylar painting made by me, and secure it to a vinyl bag by sewing through it with green vinyl rope. We then cut into it, making holes, and add appendages and limbs made of epoxy sculptural forms. We fill the inside with detritus and ephemera from KAYA's past: the body of the 18-year-old Kaya cast in resin – the preserved eternal youth; our own KAYA currency – coins we made in collaboration with the mint, Monnaie de Paris; and props from former KAYA performances. So with KAYA there is a lot of physical pressure. Through destruction, we create a new body.

When I make solo work, I am really engaging and collaborating with a glassmaker or other artisan, so the edges of authorship are fuzzy. I don't disguise any of this in my work unless I am actively playing with identity, by incorporating ghostwritten texts, staged interviews, or fictitious statements.

TWR   Among your ghostwritten texts is *What is at Hand*, a lecture you gave in 2014 at Rutgers University, which the artist Allison Katz wrote on your behalf...
KB   That text is based on my long-term

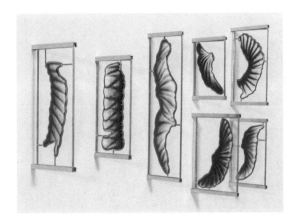

friendship with the painter Allison Katz, and the dialogue I've had with her since the start of our relationship. What is said between us in our conversations is rendered in her writing – it is a facet of our reflection on the medium specificity of painting, and the figure of a female painter. It continues my reflection on language, the way I work with text, be it ghostwritten, appropriated, collaborative, or an act of ventriloquism. For me it is also a conceptual mosaic stone that can be used to understand and frame my whole practice.

TWR   In the text, you (she) write about the ways in which your constant translation between English and German, and the destabilisation of language that happens in the process, makes you think of the slippages that happen all the time, in any form of communication.

KB   I play with these translation gaps, these glitches and mistakes. When I had my solo show *Unstable Talismanic Rendering* at Gavin Brown's Enterprise in 2014, I showed my large-scale marbled works for the first time, presenting and claiming them as semi-abstract painting. I also published a book that included *What is at Hand*. With the book, the idea was for the work to be put back into its original home – marbled paper has traditionally been used for endpapers – but to have them exist in book-form as something else, as artworks and paintings. One of the reasons *What is at Hand* is so beautiful is that we realised at a certain point during the book's production that it contained many printing errors. We decided to

make an errata page, in the form of a letter-pressed and hand-marbled insert, produced by master marbler Dirk Lange. So the mistakes make the work more valuable, they make it unique.

With works like those in the series *Unstable Talismanic Rendering*, I have attempted to create an image on a moving background. Marbling involves dripping inks and solvents in a water bath – it is very specific, alchemistic in its workings. Each drop interacts with the surface of the water as well as with all the other inks in the bath, and this particular process became a kind of collaboration with the universe. You can't manipulate the physical laws of the universe. You can't rediscover 'adhesion' or 'gravity' as an artist, but you can make marks through drops, replacing the brushstrokes that usually come from the hand of the painter. You can create, deliberately, errors of translation.

TWR   Mistakes also have a relationship to chance and indeterminacy, which seem central to your work.

KB   In *What is at Hand*, Allison wrote, 'When one drops something, the effect is a shattering; and to use the language of dropping, I might also be dropping boundaries, genres, expectations, limits, history. I am also dropping down, going low. Breaking the boundary between high and low, between painting and craft. I am moving between them.' Allison uses these sentences to create a narrative around my work, and how I arrive at each technique through the lens of painting.

After starting out with oil paint on paper,

I began painting on mylar, a transparent plastic surface, in order to question what would happen to a painting when exposed to light. I worked with UNITED BROTHERS – a collaboration between the performance artist Ei Arakawa and his brother, Tomoo Arakawa, a filmmaker who runs a tanning salon in Fukushima – to create different lighting situations for the paintings. For one body of work we created upright tanning beds – light boxes for my mylar paintings – and used tanning lights to illuminate them from within with imitation sunlight. From there I became interested in creating a painting that exists only with light, which lead me to stained glass, and creating the effect of brushstrokes with glass that mirrored marks and gestures I had made in my paintings.

TWR   Your description of the alchemy involved in marbling and your interest in light brings me to the stained glass and agate windows Sigmar Polke designed for the Grossmünster church in Zurich in 2009. You sourced fragments of refuse materials from these windows for your 2012 sculpture *Sigi's Erben*. How did that work come about?

KB   I like to think that I am literally using the trash or leftovers of a dead male artist such as Polke, like a cat licking a plate clean.

The agates became a part of that work by coincidence. The glass workshop I work with in Zurich also produced the Grossmünster church windows, and I was given access to the leftover material, so I began to work with the remaining shards of stone. You can think of my marbling works as an imitation of the geological formations of the agates. This is where the 'shattering' that Allison writes about comes in. In a sense, I had to shatter the glass by transposing the work into my marbling practice, where the marks I make are only possible through dropping. This comes full circle with my new stucco works, where, by engaging a process that is supposed to create an imitation of marble stone, my paintings rematerialise in plaster, glue, and pigment. The brushstroke once again becomes sculpted, worked on by hands in a labour- and time-intensive process of sanding, polishing, and waxing. These paintings are frozen in time. I like to call them fossil psychics.

TWR   Polke wasn't a believer, and neither was Gerhard Richter, who made the Cologne Cathedral Window. The idea of nonbelievers participating in a space of belief makes me think of the pursuit of painting itself – in the face of endless speculation on the death of the medium, there remains faith in the discipline. And in a way, churches and paintings both employ light to reference transparency and transcendence.

KB   Today, light also references the screen. Windows do not just look out onto the sun, but also into other spaces and times. Computer screens, touch screens, and smartphones allow us to communicate, as we are right now over Skype. Light can be an artificial device, it is complicated and layered. It has reframed what painting is, in terms of the digital and post-digital – even in terms of what a body is.

The end result of the marbling works I produce with the professional marbler Dirk Lange is both anachronistic and current. They look like geological patterns, but also like CGI, or anime. If you get close to a painting it reveals how messy and muddy it is, you see the spills or the hairs of the paintbrush. But with marbling, when you get closer it appears almost artificially constructed. I find it fascinating to claim this as a painting. A reversal of expectations occurs.

TWR   There is something in this element of illusion that corresponds with your interest in the occult. When DAS INSTITUT's work was exhibited at the Serpentine Sackler Gallery in 2016, the diagrammatic work of Hilma af Klint was also on display across the park, at the Serpentine Gallery. Af Klint famously engaged with spiritualism, and communicating with the beyond. Her oeuvre, which goes back to 1896, is considered by some to be the birthplace of abstraction.
KB   This has been disputed, hasn't it? You can argue that her work is the beginning of abstraction, but they were created in séances, and had a very specific function based in occult symbolism. In terms of reconsidering the beginning of Modernism, do you know what's written behind Malevich's 1915 *Black Square*? Two years ago, with an X-ray, a written sentence was discovered in the work's white border, reading 'Battle of Negroes in a Dark Cave'. Researchers wonder if Malevich's racist joke is referencing an 1897 work by French writer and humorist Alphonse

Allais, called *Combat de Nègres dans une cave pendant la nuit* (Negroes Fighting in a Cellar at Night). This discovery changes art history. Malevich as a Duchampean appropriative conceptualist? I am interested in the moment when common narratives are shaken up.

TWR   But how does the occult express itself in your work? You often evoke ghosts, phantoms, and spirits. What is useful for you in the concept of a ghost?
KB   For my first solo show in 2009 at Balice Hertling in Paris, BUYBRÄTSCHWÖRST, there wasn't much space in the gallery, so each day I rotated my paintings. First, I would show a painting in the window facing the street as an advertisement, along with a title poster that DAS INSTITUT had made for each painting. Then, on another day, I would hang the same painting, using it as a room divider, and showing it alongside a commercial for the painting that my friend Jane Jo had directed. Lastly, that painting would be exhibited on the wall, before being pulled from the show to make room for another painting. Simultaneously, I had a show at Hermes und der Pfau in Stuttgart, BUYBRÄTSCHWÖRSTGHOSTS, where I showed copies – so-called 'ghost paintings' – of the series exhibited in Paris, this time rendered on mylar, and shown alongside black-and-white Xeroxed copies of colour booklets I had made for the Paris show. Ghosts existed there.
    Allison also likes to say that my glass works

look like flat ghosts – shadowless paintings with
no body, visible, and in a sense only existing, when
illuminated. I might be going too far with this.
Maybe let's try to define a ghost. Is it something
without a shadow?

TWR Could we think about it as a version
of an original that does not live by the same laws
or rules? Or a version of an original that is able to
engage with its environment more spontaneously
or without consequence?
KB Let's take the context of my new body
of stucco work, which I call *Fossil Psychics*.
Their compositions come from my mylar paintings, so they refer to an original. But they look
trapped, like a brushstroke held by the same logic
as a fly trapped in amber. These works appear
de-deadened, as though something which didn't
have a body has returned to the physical world,
fossilised. These are fossils of ghosts. That's how
I consider this recent body of work. They display
a mark that has been multiplied and reiterated
and then turned into something physical, trapped
in stone.

TWR What made you turn to this notion of
being trapped? Was it something about the cycle
you've described of working materially and then
immaterially?
KB I think with the digital, we know that we are
working with samples, not originals. The gradient
brushstroke in my paintings – which looks like
a digital effect – becomes original again when

I sculpt it, as I do with the stuccos. I take an
alchemistic approach to revisiting traditional
models and recipes that are unknown or forgotten.
This relates to the occult, insofar as we are dealing
with secret recipes – the temperature needed for
the oven to create glass, or the chemicals required
to mix pigments, or the amount of time we must
allot to set stucco. I'm interested in dealing with
the power of the unknown, and then manipulating
its force with an awareness of contemporaneity.
I try to horizontalise universal forces such as light
or lava. I enter them into an equation: if lava is
glass, and glass is painting, then lava is painting.

A. G. L.,
Arles / New York, December 2017

Kerstin Brätsch_Ruine & *KAYA_Kovo* are
showing at Fondazione Memmo Rome until
11 November 2018.

WORKS

ART

I

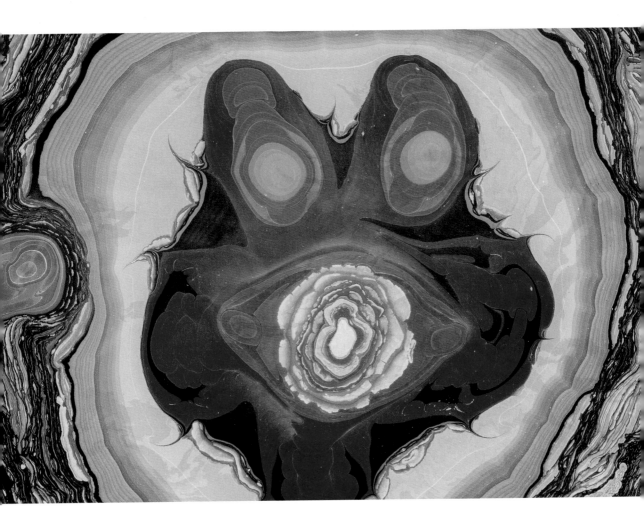

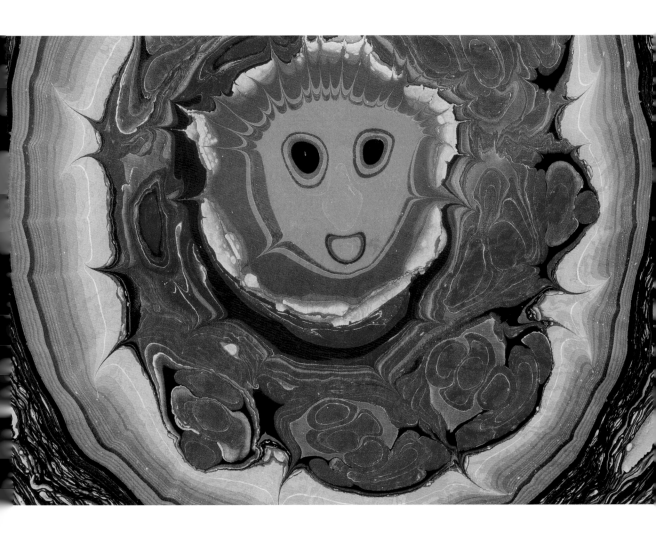

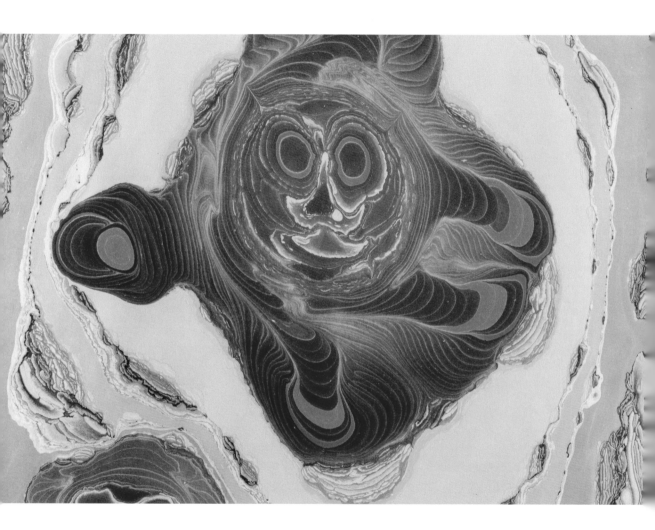

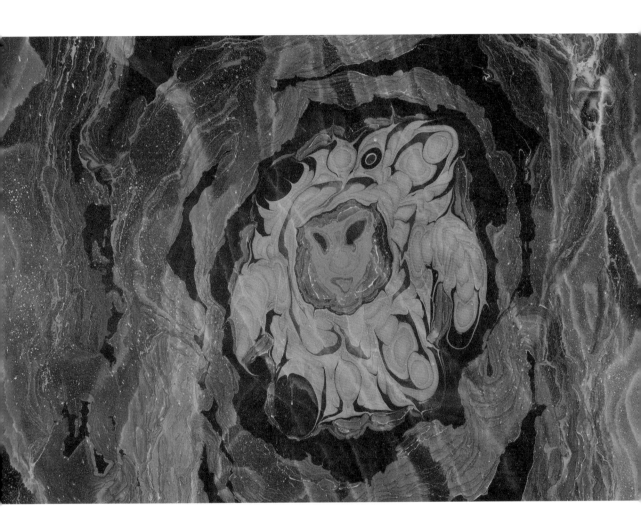

XXIII

II

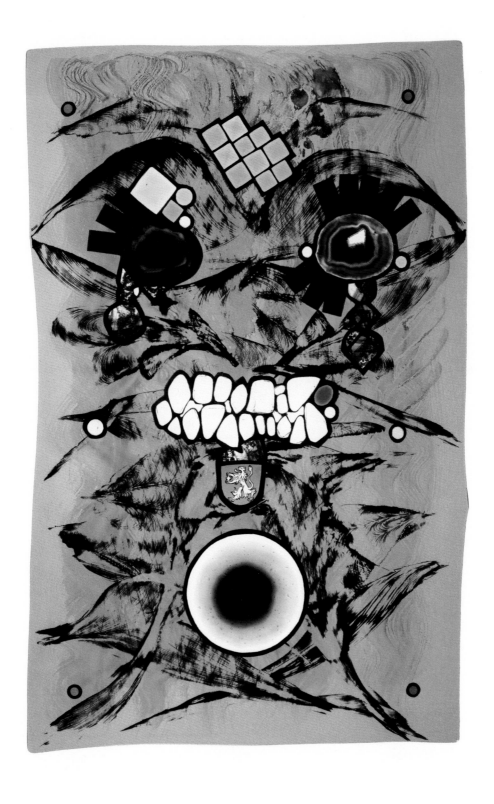

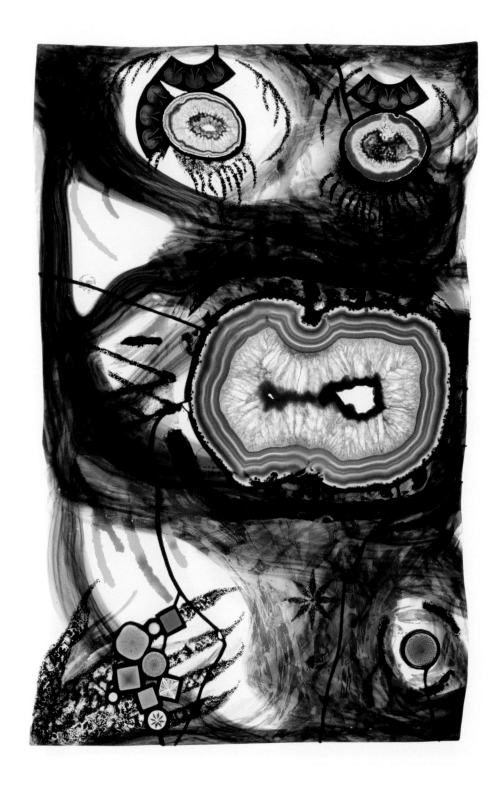

ALEX BELL

POETRY

FLORA

Under your thumb, the rouletted edge
            opens roughly a sequence
of guns tumbled like rogue fruit
            over the tilted ground.
Our pockets hot,
            we spring up raggedy and wild,
ushering days out with a blinkered skip -
            a sweet deal, a perennial favourite.

In truth, we are clean-limbed
            as Scandinavian kitchens
and the light applies itself
            in all the pretty indents.
You could wish yourself homesick,
            clearing an authentic bowl -
the butter so cylindrical,
            and rolled in salt crystals.

On the verdant astroturf, my knees
            are piston-silver and industrial.
We sleep and dream of horses
            and the night is beside itself.
Hollow, how can we hear you,
            snowy as you are, and precious,
along the rowdy outskirts? Oh.
            The slow green creepers. *Loco, loco.*

FUCHSIA

When I said *the slow green creepers,* what I meant was sex.
There was a low light, and your beard was a tree
with knotholes, into which I placed things. *Low light*
was a way of saying fire. Your veins were encrypted,
a network of stems underwater. You couldn't make sense of it.
If I called up flowers, this would signify guilt, if I described
the way they blazed at the ends of courgettes, certainly
if I made them blue and spread them over meadows.

The morning wakes up all of your confessors, carrying
in their hands their varmint hearts. This way, it is prettier.
The flowers were round-mouthed as inflatable dolls.
They were hot pink as motherfuckers.

MISSY

There is this intense heat, and you explain
that the dreams have levels, various transparencies.
In this space, you could yarn about summer, the downs,
blinking at the many rows of phalluses.

In the meaty absence of a memory,
the colours are excessive, reds and yellows feathering,
and September, that absolute boy,
arrives later than ever - so slow it is devastating.

How many russets, rotund fruits. How much doesn't happen,
and the warm ground is so very pieced together,
is warmest at its visible joins, the turning point of *after*.
This is the last ten seconds. And you are so done, so sure.

I SUPPOSE HE WAS A BIT LIKE A BULL IN A CHINA SHOP,

the Dr. said, and I couldn't remember, but there was evidence to support it.
A door opened and I walked through it. O my anecdote! My faithful sexcapade!
How it was the dearest pet. How I loved these clusters, dark and velvet.
The days were opaque with long blacks, and the long seventeenth century.
In the blind white, you can shape a memory. Look how I call up the sea,
for instance – the grey sea, set in tresses, licking at the tiny fragments of glass.
The sea, now blue and lucid. This came from nowhere. It is very clever
to make a story from just the stripped images: *there were pinstripes, a sudden euphoria.*
The euphoria never made sense. It is very clever. The man whose face you can't remember
could be any man. Sometimes, he is every man. There were pinstripes,
and a sudden euphoria. The tests said I was alright. Under the grey layer
of sea, this wondrous bumph – it is almost as though I chose this.

THE RUKARARA RIVER
SCHOLASTIQUE MUKASONGA
tr. MELANIE MAUTHNER

'La Maritza, c'est ma rivière...' sang Sylvie Vartan. 'The Maritza is my
river...' For me, who wouldn't dare sing, I would just be happy murmuring
'The Rukarara is my river...' Yes, I was actually born by the Rukarara,
yet I can't remember it; what I do remember is my mother's inconsolable
longing for it, and her memories.

The Rukarara is my river, then, although she has only ever flowed in
my imagination, and my dreams. I was only a few months old when my
family left its shores. My father worked for the local deputy chief as his
accountant and secretary, and when his employer was posted to Magi, my
father followed. Magi sits atop a high summit that towers above another
river, the Akanyaru. Beyond the Akanyaru lies Burundi. There was no
question of going down to the Akanyaru: my mother forbade all her
children, even her intrepid sons, from hurtling down the slope. She was
frightened in case we rolled all the way down the hill where crocodiles
and hippos lay in wait for us, lurking in the papyri ready to devour or
crush us, never mind the bandits from Burundi hiding in the swamps to
spy on careless children, before whisking them off in their pirogues to sell
them in Ngozi or Bujumbura to Senegalese traders who trafficked human
blood. The Akanyaru remained off-limits to my brothers and sisters and
me, a river you could see far below like a long serpent slithering among
the papyri, a river impeding any access to the outside world that must
have existed beyond the horizon and beyond Burundi – a world where
other rivers surely flowed, rivers I promised myself I would discover when
I grew up.

When my family, like so many other Tutsis, was deported to Nyamata
in Bugesera, the convoy of lorries transporting 'internally displaced
refugees' had to roll over an iron bridge to cross the Nyabarongo. But
neither the bumps nor the jolts from the vehicles on the metal roadway
could wake me as I slept in my mother's arms. Gitagata, the village of
assembly to which we were assigned, lay far from the Nyabarongo River.
I went to Lake Cyohoha to fetch water with the other girls, or, for a
solemn occasion, to the source of the Rwakibirizi whose endless abundant
flow seemed to gush miraculously from the middle of Bugesera's drought
country. The displaced people only ever spoke of Nyabarongo by cursing
her. With her earth-rich red waters, which seemed somehow to presage
misfortune, she encircled us like a rushing waterwall. This waterwall
haunted me every time I crossed the iron bridge to go back and forth to
the lycée in Kigali, because of the humiliation and violence inflicted by
the military soldiers who guarded the checkpoint. At the lycée, I learned
that for the Greeks, going to hell meant crossing a glacial gloomy river
they called the Styx; well, I knew another river that led to hell: the
Nyabarongo.

During our exile in Nyamata, my mother, Stefania, always spoke of
the Rukarara as a legendary river. When one of my little sisters fell ill –
my two youngest siblings were born in Nyamata – Stefania would lament:
'the poor little ones will never be healthy or lucky. I didn't bathe them
in the Rukarara.' We older ones born by the Rukarara, which just about
included me, were protected against innumerable illnesses, the evil curses
that we were bound to be jinxed with, and every poison with which a
jealous person might pepper our food; perhaps, Stefania hoped, we might
even be spared some of the inevitable ordeals that plague every life. For
my mother, the most effective baptism wasn't the one we had received in
church but hers, bestowed by bathing our newborn bodies in the far more
beneficial Rukarara waters.

According to Stefania, it was down on the riverbanks that the

Rukarara proffered her most bountiful riches. Her waters, since long ago used to fill troughs, had always protected our cattle from the plague epidemics that regularly afflicted the herds of Rwanda. My distraught mother would compare Bugesera's drought-ravaged land with the green, fertile, Rukarara-irrigated fields. Had my mother been able to read my father's Bible, she would have probably added the Rukarara to the list of four tributaries which, according to the Holy Scriptures, flow from the main river source in the Garden of Eden.

The Rukarara clearly concealed many mysteries. She surfaced from the earth deep in the great Nyungwe Forest, a pristine rainforest at the edge of which we had built our kraal. Nyungwe was monkey country. My mother defended our fields fiercely against their incessant raids. 'It's a useless struggle,' she said, 'they're stronger than we are but they've got their own wise elders too.' Stefania claimed to have negotiated with their chief the exact tribute we owed them from our harvests, so we had to hand it over whether we wanted to or not. She ensured that we kept to the agreement, but the monkeys always drank at the troughs before the cows did. In the evenings at storytime, Stefania told us how the king of the monkeys held court at the Rukarara's source. The monkeys kept all the other animals who might dare drink there at bay, and respected the river's purity by contenting themselves with dipping leaves in, and licking them to slake their thirst.

In 1963, nearly every one of my relatives still living in the Rukarara valley was massacred. The survivors told my mother how the river flowed blood-red with cadavers. So, I decided that from then on the Rukarara would only flow and ferry people in Stefania's stories, and that whatever happened, she would always be my enchanted river.

*

'I was born by the Rukarara River.' In the dark days of exile, I would often repeat this to myself to be sure that I had been born somewhere. The river's name gave me a more definite identity than the one the High Commission for Refugees in Bujumbura eventually deigned to inscribe on my travel pass. What an ordeal I had to endure to obtain that famous document which my brothers and sisters in exile assured me would allow me to travel and maybe even settle wherever I fancied.

Before dawn, crowds of refugees spilled onto the street and laid siege to the old colonial villa which housed the HCR offices. Some of them, mostly women carrying crying babies on their backs, waited for the bags of rice to be handed out to families, while others prided themselves on having apparently received sewing machines that would enable them to set up shop as tailors in Bujumbura's OCAF (Office des cités africaines) or Kamenge districts, thus earning the irrepressible hatred of those Burundian tailors who were already established. Most refugees came to get a mysterious attestation, an official stamped document which enabled them to obtain more attestations, that would – if, after insuperable efforts, every requirement was met, and all the necessary documents were assembled – lead the Burundian authorities to give them a residence permit, and for intellectuals and students, a travel pass which they hoped would open doors into Senegal, the Ivory Coast, or better still Belgium, even France or Germany, even the United States or, especially, Canada.

Men standing guard outside the HCR offices kept order in a desultory way, letting through those refugees who with all their shouting, swearing and jostling had managed to reach the fence, meanwhile barring at the entrance others who had spent a whole day quietly standing around. Sometimes a man emerged balancing a sewing machine on his head and people clapped, but when the rejects appeared, the crowds aimed their taunts and jeers at the high-and-mighty leaders of international bodies whom they accused of blatant partiality and intrigue, always those same plots forever dogging them. Small boys sold handfuls of peanuts wrapped in newspaper cones for two francs, and as people started to wilt and feel parched from the heat, out came Fanta orange ice cubes mixed with river water from the Mutanga, which was also Bujumbura's sewer.

I reached the infamous gate ten minutes before the offices were due to close. The guard shrugged his shoulders and let me in. Behind the ticket office grille sat an HCR employee, probably a Malian or a Senegalese, who didn't look up as he went through the usual form questions:

'Surname?'

I said Mukasonga, of course, even if it wasn't really a surname, since there aren't any in Rwanda. Your father gives you your name. It's as simple as that.

'M–U–K–A–S–O–N–G–A,' I spelled it out.

'First name?'

'Scholastique.'

He raised his head slightly. 'Is that a first name?'

'Yes, it's S–C–H–O, then it's like elastic after that.'

'OK, I'll put elastic. Born where?'

'By the Rukarara River,' I heard myself answer with exasperation. I was exhausted.

This time, the official leaned back in his chair and looked me over, gradually wondering, perhaps, whether he was dealing with a Pygmy who had just sprung from the forest, or with an arrogant Tutsi who was winding him up.

'Where's that, your Rukathingy?'

'Between Gikongoro and Cyangugu.'

'OK, I'll put Cyangugu. I know it, I've been there, it's next to Bukavu.'

The interrogation lasted right up until closing time before he ended abruptly:

'Come back in two weeks, no, a month. And bring some photos.'

I finally received that travel pass, HRC-delivered, and it was a state-lessness certificate: I was not allowed to return to Rwanda, or enter most other countries. Their embassies, when they spotted the seal on the paper indicating my refugee status, would deny me entry.

Filled with despair, I closed my eyes and took myself back to my enchanted Rukarara's riverbanks.

How could I forget her, my Rukarara? Wasn't she practically inscribed in my flesh? All I needed was to plunge my hand in my thick head of hair to feel the deep gouge of a scar running across my scalp. This scar was partly because of the Rukarara. During our regular defleaing sessions on Sunday afternoons, Stefania couldn't help but tell us children once again the origins of that wound. One of her fingers gently traced the raised skin covering my wound before she began to talk about the accident.

I had slipped out of her sight for a moment, she said, still reproaching herself. 'You never kept still even when you were just a toddler!' I had crawled as far as the field by the river. My big brother Antoine was digging a channel for the water that would irrigate our sweet potatoes. He had clearly neither seen nor heard me behind him and just as he was about to pull up a clod of earth, his hoe struck my head. My brother panicked and raced home shouting my name; he ran into my mother;

they were both frantic now and she rushed out to find me. 'I saw your open skull,' she said, 'and it wasn't blood pouring out but a white mousse, it was your brains, I saw your brains coming out.' Stefania congratulated herself on the care she had ministered by washing my wound with water from the Rukarara, then filling the gash with earth from the river bed; presumably, to speed up the healing, she had gone into the current where the river is at its deepest to haul a handful of black earth and smother it on my head from my brow to my nape. I had to stay like that for a few days. Every morning she took a close look at my wound; she was beside herself with worry until she noticed that all the earth had been swallowed and the wound had finally healed. 'That's what saved you,' she said, elated, 'the Rukarara's earth and water saved you, and that could be why you've always had something to say and you can't keep still; you'll go far, my daughter, just like the Rukarara. Antoine's hoe might well have changed the course of your thoughts!'

Sometimes, I wonder whether it is Antoine's hoe, and the Rukarara water and the earth plucked from her riverbed, that also made me a writer.

*

For a long time, the Rukarara remained the river that bordered my family's fields and kraal. I wasn't interested in what became of her further on. It was while I was writing *Our Lady of the Nile*, a novel where I imagined a girls' lycée perched on the Congo-Nile summit actually known as Ikibira, which I placed right beside the presumed source of the Nile, that I realised my little river could be connected to the great river itself.

Just as I made my character Veronica do in the novel, I tried to trace on a map the thin blue line indicating the Rukarara. She was hard to spot among the other rivulets descending the summit. Speeding south, the Rukarara flows straight out of the Nyungwe Forest, bifurcating east rather capriciously while absorbing Mushishito; then, she climbs north-eastwards to merge at last with the River Mwogo and become the Nyabarongo embracing the very heart of Rwanda in a most majestic curve – the very Nyabarongo that the Yuhi kings were unable to ford. Afterwards, when she joins the Akanyaru, she becomes known as the Akagera. Soon, boosted by the Burundian Ruvubu, the Rukarara eventually flows into Lake Victoria, and further on still, the river called Nile.

After so many peregrinations, my beloved Rukarara became the Nile! Blessed also was she as 'the most distant source of the world's greatest river', as I discovered on the Internet, learning how a team of 'explorers', a British person and two New Zealanders, had tried to go up the Nile's source in small Zodiacs. The expedition left Rosetta, near Alexandria, on 20 September 2005, hoping to reach the source ten days later: in Burundi or Rwanda? This was yet to be ascertained. Unfortunately, one explorer was killed and the other two injured in Uganda during a skirmish with rebels from the Lord's Resistance Army. Following this interruption, the expedition only started up again in March 2006. The 'explorers' resumed their journey, and when the Rukarara became too shallow for their dinghies, they continued on foot. When they came to a trickle of water spurting from a muddy silty hole at an altitude of 2428 metres, they stopped. This, the Rukarara's tiny beginning, was proclaimed 'the Nile's most distant source'. The Nile, believed up until then to be 6611 kilometres long, was now 6718 kilometres long: thanks to my Rukarara, the Nile had increased its length by 107 kilometres!

Without wishing to doubt the value of the exploits of these 'explorers' (though it does seem rather anachronistic to talk about explorers in the twenty-first century), the Rukarara had been identified as the most likely source of the Nile long before they embarked on their journey. In fact, Richard Kandt actually reached the Rukarara's source in mid-August 1898 (we don't know the exact date) and declared it then, in his book *Caput Nili*, to be the source of the Nile.[1]

I am no historian and I won't be writing a biography of Richard Kandt, fascinating though he may be, and mesmerised as he was by Rwanda and her inhabitants. I hope other scholars will take this on...

Here are some notes I gleaned while dipping into various books, just a simple bouquet cast into the Rukarara as a memento...

Richard Kantorowicz was born on 17 December 1868 in Prussian Posen, now Polish Poznań, to a family of Jewish merchants. He trained as a doctor and though he did not complete his studies, he was still given the title Doctor. Changing his name in order to assimilate, and converting to the Protestant religion (I presume he became a Lutheran), he became Doctor Richard Kandt. In 1896, he was studying anthropology, ethnology and geography in Berlin; his dream was to be an explorer, and he had learned Swahili. Is what happened next a legend? As he contemplated a statue personifying the Nile, doubtless a bearded elder, in the Vatican Museum, it seems that he decided, as so many others had done before him, that he would go in search of the great river's sources. It was Felix von Luschan, then working as an assistant at the Ethnological Museum of Berlin before he went on to invent the chromatic scale for classifying skin colour, who told him about Rwanda (his chart went from number 1 for the whitest skin to number 36 for the darkest).[2] Kandt sought in vain for sponsors to finance his expedition before finally setting off under his own steam, banking on an expected inheritance.

The aims of this solitary expedition are clearly spelled out in the first letter of *Caput Nili*. Despite the Austrian explorer Oscar Baumann asserting that the most likely source of the Nile was the Ruvubu, which flowed north from southern Burundi, Kandt was betting on the Nyabarongo:

> My journey is mapped. Once I reach the Ruvubu from the south, I need to go up to the river mouth, continue up the confluent Kagera until it joins the Kanyaru and the Nyabarongo, and only then look for the source of the stream with the greatest flow. And that could be the Nyabarongo, not the Ruvubu.

Richard Kandt arrived in Dar es Salaam in March 1897. Once he obtained the necessary permits and assembled his caravan of 140 porters, three guides, three boys and seven askaris (African soldiers), he headed off inland. He spent several months in Tabora where he bought a house. On 29 March 1898, he left for Rwanda. First of all, he visited King Yuhi Musinga, who held court at Mukingo near Gitarama. He was struck by how densely the land was populated, and especially by its Tutsi inhabitants. Their physique and demeanour fitted the portrait that Count von Goetzen, the first European to penetrate Rwanda, had penned. This was how Kandt summed up what he saw, in Caput Nili, Letter XXIII: 'A caste of Semitic or Hamite origin, whose ancestors arriving from Southern Abyssinia had conquered the vast terrain lying between the lakes... These two-metre giants reminded him of fairy tale land and legends.' Kandt evidently embraced the myth regarding the Tutsis which anthropologists had fashioned before any explorers or missionaries had even encountered them: early rumours and legends have stuck to the Tutsis like Nessus's tunic.

As he drew closer to the capital, Kandt met more and more caravans carrying tribute to the royal court, victuals and products of all sorts. On 16 May 1898, he arrived at Mukingo, site of the royal residence.

In a paragraph of rather purple prose, Kandt described all the bearers of tribute flocking and converging on the royal compound:

> A strange sight: hundreds of black silhouettes draped in bright multicoloured cloth, their lances glittering in the sun; a few litters covered with yellowing mats, long caravans bearing baskets and pots – the whole scene reminiscent of streams flowing towards a lake; clear pathlines crisscrossing crests and yellow-green slopes, leading past huts and courtyards through fields of ripe millet and banana plantations, lumbering through swamps of reeds and lazy streams, before finally pausing, as a giant fat multicoloured serpent might, around the outer fence of the Residence...

After a few evasive statements from the Court dignitaries, Kandt was ushered into the royal residence for an audience with the mwami. Although local advice had indicated to Kandt that Yuhi Musinga was supposedly sixteen years old, to his stupefaction the person to whom he was presented was, he wrote:

> a man of about forty with copper-coloured skin and half-closed sleep-filled eyes. Nevertheless, he wore royal attire: a headband roughly twenty centimetres wide made of white pearls with six decorative zigzag lines of pink pearls. Large tufts of long white silky monkey hair draped his neck from the upper edge of this strange head dress. From its lower edge hung around fifteen tresses, artistically plaited with red and white pearls, covering most of his face to his top lip. He wore a short pagne of fine tanned hide over his buttocks; and in front, the leather against his skin was folded twice over his genitals, its upper border stitched to finery made up of hundreds of rows of tiny pearls. Twenty plaited snake skin straps hung from the hide's lower rim... and several rows of pearls were tied around his waist, while from his body hung ten to fifteen woven bangles each dangling three white pearls. He wore a necklace made from slender tubes of pearls... On his chest were quantities of amulets, most no bigger than little flacons, wrapped in plaited covers decorated with zigzags of bicoloured pearls. On his arms, he wore between 150 and 200 copper or brass bracelets, most of which bore a large blue pearl or tiny bells forged from the same metals. Nearly 100 wire rings encircled his ankles which accounted, as previously mentioned, for his lumbering gait.

Conversation was struck up with a dignitary thanks to the intermediary of Kandt's cook's wife. The king did not join in, he was happy simply to nod his head now and then. Kandt asked for food supplies for his caravan. Promises were made. After fifteen minutes, exasperated by the lack of interest shown by his hosts, Kandt took his leave and made for his camp where his troops were relieved to see him. Later, once Kandt had gained Musinga's trust, he would discover that the pseudo-mwami was Mpamarugamba, a powerful leader of the Ryangombe cult. He was the Spirit Master capable of countering harmful forces said to be brought by strange white visitors, and thus it was his duty to protect the royal person-age whose youth rendered him vulnerable.

The Rwandans took their time before providing the requested provisions. But faced with this white man's impatience, the royal court finally acquiesced, and Kandt set off again towards his planned destination: the source of the Nile.

He proceeded through a densely populated region covered in banana trees. Other trees were few and far between, except for some tall solitary ficus trees which he called 'fig trees', 'dedicated', he noted, 'to the memory of deceased chiefs'. After 'fourteen days of pleasant walking', he reached the confluence of the two rivers that would engender the Nyabarongo: the Mwogo and the Rukarara. These two rivers were quite distinct:

> Like a shaky exhausted old man, the Mwogo comes up from the south snaking through swamps... while the Rukarara leaps over stones and tree stumps, clear and fresh as wild hurtling youth.

The Rukarara's flow, Kandt noted, was far greater than the Mwogo's. So, it was the Rukarara's course which he needed to follow to reach what could then be proclaimed to be the Nile's source. This somewhat displeased Kandt, because the Rukarara's source was assumed to lie in 'horrifyingly impenetrable jungle'. However, the expedition proceeded along the river's increasingly steep-sided course. The hamlets, so numerous up until then, became more scattered, and by the fifth day they disappeared completely as the caravan entered 'the dark pristine forest'. The cold took him by surprise, and his expedition team even more so: his boy woke Kandt up in a panic to show him the water bucket covered 'with a layer of two-centimetre-thick ice'. By morning, the grass and trees were white with frost. The following night, Kandt left his tent to bed down between two roaring fires.

Kandt eventually reached his goal in mid-August:

> At this spot, the Rukarara was but a mere brook 30 centimetres across spurting from a gorge with no issue, buried in thick vegetation. The next day, I ventured forth with a native and some of my men. It was most difficult. It took us nearly an hour to advance 500 metres. But with our axes and machetes, we managed to hack our way through, plunging into the swamp up to our waists, crawling on all fours in freezing water, straggling up the gorge. Several hours later, drenched and exhausted from our efforts, smothered from head to toe in mud, we reached a small hollow deep in the narrow pass where the source seeps from the earth not in a froth but drop by drop.

In fact, according to the tourist map spread out before me, the source that Kandt had just discovered was not the Rukarara's but that of its smaller tributaries. The map shows it as Source de Kandt, and a bit further north, the actual Rukarara source is starred *Source du Nil.

I shall leave Dr Richard Kandt to his fate, he who long before the missionaries was the first European to live in Rwanda, a botanist and cartographer, and to the German authorities their unofficial citizen, until in 1907 he became an official imperial resident, a backer of Musinga's reign; a founder of Kigali, where you can visit his house now restored as the city's Botanical Museum; on leave in Germany when war broke out, then called up and gassed on the Eastern Front, only to die on 29 April

I prefer to imagine Richard Kandt at his camp: night has fallen; the songs and laughter and cries of his exhausted porters have gradually subsided after a long day's trek; he has bathed in water his boy has prepared for him, he has eaten rather absent-mindedly the filet of antelope he killed the previous evening, he tries as he does every night to read a page of Nietzsche whom he so admires, but his thoughts keep bringing him back to these troubling encounters he has been having since he arrived in Rwanda, and which are now interrupting the words of Zarathustra. Who were these people whose 'discretion, reserve, solemnity, and blasé attitude' so contrasted with the exuberance and lavish welcome he had received up until then? And why did the young court dandies disdain the embellished silk fabrics, 'the long Arab coats, the short multicoloured jackets embroidered with rich silver filigree', even the red Prussian Hussar uniforms he offered them, preferring instead 'unicoloured cloth if possible, with discreet subdued motifs'? Were these the barbarians whom Kandt's caravan men had mocked, who knowing nothing of the worth of these precious silks opted instead for plain cottons? Or were they more akin to that aristocrat, who when told of 'a magnificent Parisian treasure' by Kandt, replied that the jewel might be very fine but was more suited 'to a banker's wife'?

And as he marvelled at the royal residence spanning the hilltop before him, why did Kandt feel like a pilgrim after a long and arduous journey to his holy city?

> At last, we have scaled our final hill and from the summit, we can see the sovereign's residence on the opposite crest. It is a vast complex of rondavels with tight interlacing plaited fences encircling large courtyards. Ficus trees serve as fence posts, they have taken root and their broad leafy canopies give an agreeable colour to the whole ensemble. All sorts of huts form a vast circle on the hilltops and slopes, the bigger ones are for dignitaries, the smaller ones for vassals... But my eye is drawn always to the royal residence itself, leaving me with a strange impression of familiar images awoken from vague memories without my being able to place them. While the caravan halts for a much-needed short pause to regroup, I delve inside my mind and feel uneasy as faces reappear as if waking after a long slumber from a buried corner of my brain...
>
> And then, I am flooded with this feeling which has assailed me several times during this trip before particularly odd scenes; the sombre oppressive sensation of déjà vu as if I had already lived through all this in another forgotten life.

When at last he reached the royal compound, it was a medieval fortified castle he entered:

> And deep in the heart of Africa, my imagination fires up again breathing new life to knights' pennants and pages as if they had arisen from engravings or long-lost books.

But to Richard Kandt, 'these vague memories, this sombre oppressive sensation of déjà vu' that he felt again and again for these 'giant Watutsis' – being, as a white man and moreover a citizen of the German Empire, naturally convinced of his superiority – were but the mere distorting mirror through which Europeans would continue to perceive Rwanda and her inhabitants. The greatest misfortune to befall Rwandans was to live by the sources of the Nile, where since antiquity the myth of an unspoilt Eden, a lost and unreachable paradise, has taken root. Apparently the phrase 'Caput Nili quaerere' – 'to search for the source of the Nile' – was for the Romans an expression meaning 'to seek the impossible'. Rwanda was the last blank spot on the map of an Africa which explorers were giving over to colonisation. Perhaps, this ultimate *terra incognita* still concealed the last wonders, the final mysteries, of a continent desecrated and sullied everywhere else with everyday, humdrum colonialism. The existence of the Nile's sources allowed people, if not to actually discover them, to invent beings just emerged from the land of legend, a quasi-primeval race who would bewitch anew an Africa whom industry and commerce had defiled. And who better to fill that role but the statuesque Tutsis, with their finely chiselled features and imposing bearing... There, where mere Rwandans dwelled, people saw the Pharoah's Egyptian progeny, the Queen of Sheba's Ethiopian descendants, wandering Jews from the ten lost tribes of Israel, and Christian Copts whose memories would just need to be jogged...

So, was Dr Richard Kandt, formerly Kantorowicz and Jewish, an intellectual and lone explorer, and for all these reasons up against the soldiers' and missionaries' contempt[3] – was he on the verge of recognising in these fascinating and perplexing Tutsis his long-lost wandering brothers, so far yet so near... And within Mukingo's huts, who knows which ghost from Jerusalem?

*

I am both relieved and slightly disappointed that nowadays, the Rukarara is just considered an ordinary river. They have built a hydroelectric power station that does not seem to meet everyone's expectations, but people living near the river can still hope to benefit one day from the progress electricity brings: school pupils will be able to study by lamplight, young intellectuals to recharge their mobile phones and the wealthy to spend their evenings with friends in front of the television tucking into kebabs and beer served by a charming young Rwandan.

The source of the Nile itself is within the reach of every tourist. Tour operators will provide an itinerary for how to get there. You start from the tea factory at Gisovu, but it is best to phone twenty-four hours ahead and book a guide. People recommend going up to Gisovu from Kibuye on Lake Kivu, rather than from Gikongoro. From Gisovu, a path takes you to the source (the actual source, not Kandt's source) in just under an hour. They say the walk there presents no difficulty.

I am packing my suitcase. I have bought some walking shoes. This time, I have made my decision: next year will see me by the Rukarara. Caput Nili!

1. It is a real shame for Rwandans and for all those interested in Rwanda, and for those like me who do not know German, that *Caput Nili, eine empfindsame Reise zu den Quellen des Nils* (Dietrich Reimer Verlag, Berlin, 1904) has not yet been translated or published in French. Only a few excerpts are available, thanks to Bernard Lugan, in the journal *Études rwandaises* (volume XIV, October 1980, Université nationale du Rwanda). I would like to thank my friend Henri Moncomble, Professor of German, who translated Letters I, XXIII and XXVI for me. [All English translations here are by Melanie Mauthner.]

2. Felix Ritter von Luschan's chromatic scale was made up of thirty-six squares of opaque glass: patches of human skin least exposed to the sun were compared to the glass squares. According to his scale, there were thirty-six skin types that could be classified into six distinct categories:

I	1 to 5	Very fair Celtic type
II	6 to 10	Fair European
III	11 to 15	Dark European
IV	16 to 21	Mediterranean
V	21 to 28	Olive-skinned
VI	29 to 36	Black

3. In his biography of Monseigneur Classe, *Un audacieux pacifique* (Collection Labigerie, Grands Lacs, Namur, 1948), Father A. Van Overschelde draws freely on anti-semitic rhetoric to describe Kandt: 'Richard Kandt was a highly intelligent Jew, with a poetic bent, small, stunted and olive-skinned. The bile that gave rise to his complexion did not only course beneath his skin: he was nasty. His build and perhaps his age-old habits did not dispose him to be forthright. He was a smooth operator who excelled at undercover step by step plotting in a manner reminiscent of a feline.'

SEA MONSTERS
CHLOE ARIDJIS

FICTION

Imprisoned on this island, I would say, *Imprisoned on this island*. And yet I was no prisoner and this was no island.

During the day I'd roam the shore, aimlessly, purposefully, and in search of digressions. The dogs. A hut. Boulders. Nude tourists. Scantily clad ones. Palm trees. Palapas. Sand sifting umber and adrenaline. The waves' upward grasp. A boat in the distance, its throat flashing in the sun. The ancient Greeks created stories out of a simple juxtaposition of natural features, my father once told me, investing rocks and caves with meaning, but there in Zipolite I did not expect any myths to be born.

Zipolite. People said the name meant Beach of the Dead, though the reason for this was debated – was it because of the number of visitors who met their end in the treacherous currents, or because the native Zapotecs would bring their dead from afar to bury in its sands? Beach of the Dead: it had an ancient ring, ancestral, commanding both dread and respect, and after hearing about the unfortunate souls who each year got caught in the riptide I decided I would never go in beyond where I could stand. Others said Zipolite meant Lugar de Caracoles, place of seashells, an attractive thought since spirals are such neat arrangements of space and time, and what are beaches if not a conversation between the elements, a constant movement inwards and outwards. My favourite explanation, which only one person put forward, was that Zipolite was a corruption of the word *zopilote*, and that every night a black vulture would envelop the beach in its dark wings and feed on whatever the waves tossed up. It's easier to reconcile yourself with sunny places if you can imagine their nocturnal counterpart.

Once dusk had fallen I would head to the bar and spend hours under its thatched universe, a large palapa on the shores of the Pacific decked with stools, tables and miniature palm trees. It was where all boats came to dock and refuel, syrup added to cocktails for maximum sweetness, and I'd imagine that everything was as artificial as the electric blue drink; that the miniature palm trees grew fake after dusk, the chlorophyll struggling and the life force gone from the green, that the wooden stools had turned to laminate. Sometimes the hanging lamps would be dimmed and the music amplified, a cue for the drunks and half drunks to clamber onto the tables and start dancing. The shoreline ran through every face, destroying some, enhancing others, and at moments when I'd had enough reminders of humanity I would look around for the dogs who like everyone else at the beach came and went according to mood. A curious snout or a pair of gleaming eyes would appear on the fringes of the palapa, take in the scene, and then, most often, finding nothing of interest, retire once more into darkness.

Before long, it became apparent that the bar in Zipolite was a meeting place for fabulists, and everyone seemed to concoct a tale as the night wore on. One girl, a painter with cartoon lips and squinty eyes, said her boyfriend had suffered a heart attack on his yacht and been forced to drop her off at the nearest port since his wife was about to be helicoptered in with a doctor. In more collected tones, a tall German explained to everyone that he was a representative of the German Society for Protection Against Superstition, or Deutsche Gesellschaft Schutz vor Aberglauben – he wrote the name in tiny German script on a sheet of rolling paper for us to read – and had been sent to Mexico after a stint in Italy. An actress from Zacatecas no one had heard of insisted she was so famous that a theatre, a planet, and a crater on Venus had been named after her.

And you, someone would ask, noticing how intently I listened, What brought you here? I had run away, I told them, I'd run away from home.
Are your parents evil? No, not at all...
... I was in Zipolite with a boy. I'd run away, mainly, because of a boy.
And where was this boy?
Good question.
And *who* was this boy?
Another good question.

But that, too, was only half the truth. I had also come here because of the dwarfs. However fantastical it now seemed, I was here with Tomás, a boy I hardly knew, in search of a troupe of Ukrainian dwarfs. And if I stopped to think about it for more than a few instants, the situation was almost entirely my fault. It was therefore not surprising that calming thoughts were hard to come by. No calm, but a profound numbness, as if stuck halfway through a dream, a dream I didn't seem able to exit – and yet strangely, the realisation didn't trouble me.

The palapa held out the promise of one thing while the animated conversation and gaudy cocktails delivered another, and once I'd had enough I would return to my hammock through the sifting black of the beach and watch shadows advance and recede, never certain as to who or what they were. Sometimes I would see Tomás walk past, his shadow easy to pluck out from the rest, and though he kept a certain distance I recognised him instantly, tall and slender with a jaunty gait, almost like a puppet of wood and cloth slipped over a giant hand.

At some point I would have to explain to myself and to any witnesses how it was that I had ended up in Zipolite with him.

He had started out as a snag, a snag in the composition; from one moment to the next, there was no other way of putting it, he had begun to appear in my life back in the city. And since all appearances are ultimately disturbances, this disturbance needed investigating.

I didn't even particularly like him at first, intrigued would be a better word. He was a sliver of black slicing through the so-called calm of the morning. I still remember most details, the pinkish light that spread over the street, painting the tips of trees and the uppermost windows, the shops shut, as well as the curtains on houses, and the only person I'd encountered within this stillness was the elderly organ grinder in his khaki uniform, seated on a bench polishing his barrel organ with a red rag before heading to the Centro. *Harmonipan Frati & Co. Schönhauser Allee 73 Berlin* read the gold letters down the side, but the organ grinder himself lived in La Romita, the poorer section of La Roma, though he always came to the plaza near my house to polish his instrument, preparing it for a social day outside the cathedral. None of his kind had ever been to Europe but they carried Europe in their instrument, their uniform, and their nostalgic, old-fashioned manner.

And it was as he sat there on the bench beginning his day that I saw another figure appear: a young man in black, tall and slender with a pale face and hair shooting out in twenty directions, who walked up to the *organillero* and held out a coin – I assumed it was a coin, all I saw was the glint of a small object transferred between hands – and continued on his way. The elderly man nodded in surprised gratitude; he was probably used to receiving alms when music was produced, not silence, and here, out of nowhere, first thing in the morning, had come this offering.

Despite having to catch the school bus at 7.24 I followed the new person as he hurried down streets parallel to the ones I normally took, past *mozos* sweeping the streets before their employers awoke and tramps curled up in the porticos of grand houses beginning to uncurl. But once he turned off into Puebla my inner map cried out and I swerved round and retraced my steps in a hurry, arriving just in time to board my bus at the junction where Monterrey meets Alvaro Obregón. The quiet of the streets vanished the moment I stepped onto this travelling ship of the wide awake, wide awake thanks to the gang of new wave Swedes at the back. There were four of them, three boys and a girl – sister to one – and they colonised the final row with their blondeness and asymmetrical haircuts, always one strand eclipsing an eye, and trousers rolled up just enough to reveal their pointy lace-up shoes, but above all they colonised the bus with their stereo, for they asserted themselves, communicated almost entirely, through their music – Yazoo, Depeche Mode, the Human League, Soft Cell and Blancmange – and it was in this way, after the first glimpse of Tomás, that I was launched into the day.

In Zipolite the sun seared the sand, and the heat particles, free to roam where they pleased, dissipated in the air. Yet our Mexico City was situated in a valley circled by mountains. High pressure weather systems, weakened air flows, rampaging ozone and sulphur dioxide levels, basin geography: a perfect convergence of factors, said the experts, for thermal inversion. Ours was a world of refraction, where light curved, producing mirages, and sound curved too, amplifying the roar of airplanes near the ground. And each time an event in Mexico challenged the natural order of things, which was often, my parents and I called it thermal inversion.

Thermal inversion whenever a politician stole millions and the government covered it up, thermal inversion when an infamous drug trafficker escaped from a high security prison, thermal inversion when the director of a zoo turned out to be a dealer in wild animal skins and two lion cubs went missing. But the real thing existed too, and on some days the air pollution was so fierce I'd return from school with burning eyes, and everyone from taxi drivers to news presenters complained about the *esmog* but the government did nothing. The clouds over our city were of an immovable slate, granite and lead, and only the year before migratory birds had dropped dead from the sky – exhaustion, the officials had said, they died of exhaustion, but everyone knew the poisoned air had cut their journeys short, lead in the form of dispersed molecules rather than compacted into a bullet.

At first I thought thermal inversion was possible only in the city, and then I thought it possible in Zipolite only in the form of the Swiss biker in black leather – his movements constricted by his tight leather shorts and leather vest, he spent all day drinking beer on the sand, his black leather cap surely a magnet for heat, and never entered the water. Yet I soon began dreaming of other forms of inversion, for instance if I could replace Tomás with Julián, my current best friend. Yes, if Julián were there instead, I might have more perspective, somehow, on the given situation, or at the very least a genuine partner in crime, be it in silence or conversation.

But Julián was back in the city. He was back in the city, on the top floor of the Covadonga, that was his address, the large elegant billiard hall near the corner of Puebla and Orizaba. The waiters at Covadonga would have cut funny figures in Zipolite, like penguins at the beach in their black waistcoats and bowties and the imperturbable expression of men who'd seen a great deal over the decades; the place had been around since the 1940s and some of them, according to my father, had worked there since their youth. On the ground floor lay the billiard tables, on the first floor a restaurant, on the second floor a dance salon. Julián lived on the third, used for storage and visiting musicians. He'd become friends with Eduardo, one of the waiters, and, having nowhere to go after deferring university and falling out with his boyfriend, brother, and father, was offered the space on the condition that he vacate whenever the owner, who lived in Spain, came to Mexico, and for any trios or duos or solo musicians who happened to pass through.

The top rooms contained an assembly of half-living objects: foldout chairs and tables, some in stacks against the wall, a gas canister hooked up to a four-burner cooker, its stark metal frame like a vertebra, and a red cooler with the letters CERVEZA CORONA in blue. The back room had a cot, where Julián slept under a pile of tablecloths, surrounded by boxes of folded linen and fluorescent tubes. A defunct disco ball, missing most of its square mirrors, hung from the ceiling; the only light was the one that glowed through the windows shaped like portholes. In these rooms I'd spend many an hour with Julián and his stereo, a General Electric that guzzled size D batteries. In one corner was parked a guitar with Camel insignia, for which his mother had smoked her way through two hundred cartons of cigarettes; with the coupons and a bit of cash she had bought it for her son one Christmas. He seldom played it, however, since he felt she had died for that guitar.

The CORONA cooler was kept well stocked, usually with Sol or Negra Modelo, and we'd sit back in the foldout chairs and paint the future, the details changing each time, as we wandered side by side through a landscape of perhapses. Perhaps he would become a sculptor, or a rock musician. Perhaps I would become an astronomer or an archaeologist. Perhaps he would partner up with the owner of the Covadonga and one day inherit the place and its four floors. Several days a week I would walk over after school, especially when my parents weren't home, and sensed at moments that this was the closest I would ever come to having a sister. Sometimes we'd carry two chairs out to the narrow balcony, from which there was a view of the spire and rose window of the Sagrada Familia, our neighbourhood church, though like many city views ours was bisected at different heights by a tangle of cables. If the day was rainy or overly polluted we'd bring the chairs back inside and listen to the radio. One station played songs from England and Julián kept the dial there, though every now and then he'd swivel it over to a pirate station that offered unofficial news, a quick reality check before we returned to our fantasies, and every now and then he'd slip in a cassette and we'd listen to the same track over and over, usually Visage's 'Fade to Grey' or the Cure's 'Charlotte Sometimes', and we'd stop talking and just listen, letting all that had sunken well up inside.

*

When I was younger we kept an aquarium, a slice of sea in a corner of my father's study. It lived half in shadow since the curtains were kept semi-closed

– too much sunlight encouraged algal bloom – and anyway, night was when it came alive. Whenever I couldn't sleep I'd go sit and watch the aquatic spider writing her dreams into the water and the clownfish zigzagging across the tank and others pulsing by in their silvery blue waistcoats. During moments of extreme restlessness I'd be soothed by the fact total inactivity did not exist, even at three in the morning there was something in motion, a plan being executed at the most micro of levels. Someone once said that the dream is the aquarium of the night, but to my mind night was the aquarium of the dream, with our visions framed within it. And then came the moment when the last fish died. My mother standing over the tank trying to ladle it out with a green net. As I watched from a nearby sofa, all was unleashed and for an instant it felt like the entire universe was focusing on our home. The phone rang. A knock on the front door. The fax machine trilling. A caterwaul from our neighbour Yolanda's house. Dogs howling from rooftops. Klaxons and sirens in the distance. Everything spoke at once, a collective dirge for the dead fish.

Whenever I felt disheartened or defeated I'd recall my father's words, words he would repeat long after we'd stored the aquarium at the back of a closet and filled it with papers. Remember, he'd say, society is like a fish tank, only less beautiful to watch. The structure is not so different, however: here we have the shy fish who spend their lives hiding between the rocks, missing out on moments both important and trivial, then the gregarious types who crisscross the water in search of company or adventure, always on the move without knowing where they're headed, and then the curious ones who hover close to the surface, first in line for food but also first should any hand or paw plunge in.

Yet his words lost meaning before the ocean, here there was no visible order or structure, only one great matriarch, vast and indifferent as a cathedral. And that indifference had to be reckoned with, it had to be measured and addressed if there was to be any interaction between humans and ocean. From my first day in Zipolite I noticed the system of flags – green, yellow and red – a code imposed on the ocean's movements: the ocean produced waves and we responded with triangles of colour that mediated between us, rising up like strange pointy flowers on tall poles in the sand. No farther in than your knees, some said, because like everything dead, this beach and its waves will try to suck you under.

From Zipolite I now imagined my parents plastering my image to lampposts, my face added to the missing dog posters in our neighbourhood. *Se busca Azlán. Se busca Bonifacio. Se busca Chipotle.* Each time I saw one I would fantasise about finding the animal – for the animal's sake, for the owner's sake, for the reward. But no image was permanent. These posters would start out vivid, inked with the owner's nervous expectation, but as the days went by the hope and colour would be drained from them and one morning they'd be torn down by a man in beige who went around removing expired notices. Some of the animals I recognised but others must have spent their entire lives indoors; I had a pretty good sense of most of the dogs in La Roma, many of whom were brought to the plaza to run, others taken out by the neighbourhood dogwalker. Other sights: a pair of Rottweilers jumping up and down behind the wire mesh of their gate, two dark masses springing as if on a trampoline, fiercely guarding the only territory they knew, and our local priest, who would change into trainers at night and walk his white Maltese through the dirty streets.

The dogs in Zipolite may have been safe from city woes yet all day long they wandered up and down the beach, as if scavenging for something not provided by the landscape. They took the beach's temperature, gauged its mood, sussed out every new arrival. A ragbag of breeds, none were one solid colour but rather a patchwork of two or three tones. Some had faces like masks, pure black interrupted by a tan snout or a set of golden eyebrows, others resembled wolves or oversized cats. One had a splash of German shepherd though he was much smaller in size and nowhere near as regal; these dogs were more like courtiers but even among courtiers there must be a king, and the leader of the pack, as far as I could tell, was this unabashed shepherd mongrel, average in height but lofty in carriage, whom the others followed around and turned to for cues.

From early on I noticed the dogs didn't take to Tomás. They would avoid him and snarl when he came too close. Yet he didn't pay much attention, and when they first approached, after all we were new scents on the beach, he yelled *¡Lárganse!* and kicked the air near their heads. I'd often share my snacks with them, whatever I happened to have, which was never very much, and as a result the motley congregation would come sit by my side. How had I ended up in Zipolite preferring the company of these dogs to the person I'd run away with, I'd ask myself, while the sea continued to write and erase its long ribbon of foam.

JENNY OFFILL   INTERVIEW

In *Dept. of Speculation* (2014), Jenny Offill's second novel, the narrator is distracted from writing a second novel by her family, but also by a bedbug infestation and a job ghostwriting a history of the space programme for a failed astronaut. In *Last Things* (1999), Offill's debut, eight-year-old Grace, homeschooled by her increasingly erratic mother, learns mainly about the formation of the universe and the insects that will remain after mammalian extinction. The very large and the very small, along with philosophy and history, poetry and religion, recontextualise – for Offill's characters and for her readers – the ordinary and not so ordinary events of domestic life. *Dept. of Speculation* consists of fragments, most of them well under half a page, that relate the narrator's trajectory from unattached young woman to wife and mother; interspersed with these are tenets of Buddhism and Manichaeism, self-help jargon and quotations from Rilke, Simone Weil, Hesiod and Antarctic explorers.

Offill began writing *Last Things* shortly out of college, while on a Stegner Fellowship from Stanford University, and it was published eight years later. Since then, she has taught writing at universities in New York and North Carolina, and in 2019 she will take up a post as a visiting writer at Vassar College. She is the author of four children's books and co-editor, with Elissa Schappell, of two essay anthologies. *Dept. of Speculation* – shortlisted for the Folio Prize, the Pen/Faulkner Award and the L.A. Times Fiction Award – was praised widely for the originality of its form and compared to works published around the same time by Elena Ferrante, Sheila Heti, Ben Lerner and Rachel Cusk, for its seeming autofictionality and its preoccupation with the difficulty of combining mother-hood, or any intimate relationship, with creative work. 'My plan was never to get married. I was going to be an art monster instead [...] art monsters only concern themselves with art, never mundane things,' the narrator remembers, once she is married and deeply concerned with mundane things.

Offill is now working on her third novel, *American Weather*. Its librarian protagonist finds her limited sphere of concern widening to include climate change and global politics. I interviewed Offill, who lives in upstate New York, in a narrow French restaurant on Manhattan's Upper East Side. It was late February, one week after the Parkland school shooting and the day that Trump was meeting survivors in Washington D.C. The topic of climate change came up almost immediately: the temperature was in the early twenties, unnervingly warm after weeks of below zero. (I later discovered that it was the warmest February day on record.) After the interview we walked through a busy Central Park. Offill was totally engaging, at once serious and very funny, with the same black humour evident in her novels. Over several kinds of cheese, we began by discussing our different experiences teaching, and the usefulness – or otherwise – of having mentors or peers read writing-in-progress.   HANNAH ROSEFIELD

TWR   Do you show your work to people as you're writing?

JO   I tend to be someone who wants to write the whole thing before I show it to anyone. It's not ideal, because I'm also really, really slow. It's such a private language, when you're in the middle of a book, and there's an associational, dream logic to the way I write. Donald Barthelme talks about the 'not-knowingness' of writing fiction. I live in that state for many years, and then it can be a course correction, when you do show it to somebody. I never really want suggestions exactly, but there is a fear that maybe it won't make sense to anyone else. At the same time, sharing my work too much diffuses whatever mystery there is for me in the writing of it, and then I stop being able to hear what I'm doing.

TWR   I recently heard an interview with Claire Messud, where she said that when she's teaching fiction workshops, she always asks her students to describe what they see in their peers' work, rather than making suggestions about what should change.

JO   I made a joke in my workshop that I would get them all T-shirts that said 'I wanted to know more'. The nature of workshops, the way that they're structured, means they lean towards the writer adding things: OK, we don't know enough about this person, we don't know enough about this event, can you show us more clearly what this scene is about? But if you're someone who is trying to move to a more pared-down language, or language that is trying to do things at a couple of different levels at the same time, the workshop environment can be difficult. So I try to teach my students to read at the line level, because I think that's what's helpful: to start thinking about what they're writing line by line, as well as the bigger picture. I'm also always trying to make them read things in different genres: poetry or essays or non-fiction or primary sources from science or anthropology. I want them to get a sense of the strangeness of language. It reminds you that there are all these different ways in which you can create density and give a vital feeling to the words on the page.

TWR   You talk about using a pared-down language. When you're writing or revising, how do you think about what to remove?

JO   The one dictum that I've always gone back to is Italo Calvino: revision as 'the subtraction of weight'. The Olympics are on right now, and when you watch the really, really good skaters, they make it look easy, and they make you think you could skate like that. There's some kind of fluidity... and for me the subtraction of weight is also the subtraction of the stagecraft, and the sweat. I want my work ultimately to feel beautiful and mysterious, and also to make people wonder how it was done. Because that's what I like in books. I like to wonder how it was done. Sometimes you can figure out certain things, ways a writer might use transitions, for example. Or I was talking in one of my classes about Denis Johnson. You're always told as a writer that you should move towards the specific, but actually in *Jesus' Son* Johnson has an amazing vagueness that's really radiant and strange. There's a passage where he's in a Polish neighbourhood, wandering around, and he says something like, 'They have that fruit with the light on it, they have that music you can't find.' That's all he says, but to me, it gives a feeling of... I know it's a stand-in for the limits of language itself. I'm always interested in how you get to the point where you can't say the thing you're trying to express. It's what every mystical tradition is interested in: at a certain point language falls away, and how can you go to that point, and participate in that space between what you're trying to say and what can land on the page? Vagueness, in the hands of a master, is one way you can do that, but of course it only works if you also show that you can be incredibly particular. *Then* you can say something that's incredibly abstract.

TWR   When you were writing *Dept. of Speculation*, did it start big and then you cut it down?

JO   No, I never start big. I write these little things, and I don't know how they're going to fit together. I was just reading Frank O'Hara's 'Personism' manifesto, where he says you just have to go on nerve. That's what it is: I know things go together, but I have no idea how. I just know they have a sort of... a slightly magnetic quality. They're not sticking, but if you hold them together, there's a tiny charge. So I'm just trying to figure out where the things go.

TWR   When you say things, do you mean the fragments of the novel? Or phrases?

JO   It might not be at the phrase level. It's more like: I have this section about a reporter coming back from the space station, and I also have a thing about explorers, and I have a moment with a mother and a child in a bathtub. With *Dept.*, I had all these fragments, but I didn't know whether there was any story there, because for a long time I resisted having the break in the novel [the revelation of the main character's husband's affair]. I just felt like, why tell that same story? The larger things, the structuring, point of view and so on, is more intuitive. When I was writing the novel, I changed the point of view intuitively, and the whole time I was thinking I would have to go back and fix it. But your writing brain is much smarter than your analytical brain. And then at a certain point I realised that the way I was using pronouns echoed exactly the emotional distance between the narrator and her husband. So I started moving the fragments to reflect the pronouns, and then I could write the end, because I knew I wanted the novel to go back to 'I' and 'you' right at the end. But I also knew that I had to put several lines before that final fragment that are just descriptions, no pronouns at all. It was the same with the page that just says 'soscared', over and over... I had that originally, but I didn't know where it went. Then I realised: that's the transition point between different points of view.

TWR   Because you didn't want to change the point of view too suddenly?

JO   Right. It shouldn't feel jarring, but if you're not brave enough in the way you do it, it can feel like a mistake. So the problem is: how do you make everything feel as intentional as it is, but still have that lightness that Calvino talks about? Those two things seem as if they're working against each other. Some people ask me whether all the parts in the novel could be rearranged. No! Not at all. I know what goes on in between the different fragments, and I didn't put that in the book because I wanted to play with form. I also feel like the character's mind is galloping along, and so there were places where I wanted visually, in the text, to give you a place to rest. Certain scenes are slowed down for that reason, or there's text from other places for that reason. *I* like to be in the character's head, but I could imagine that some people would be thinking *Jesus, I need a break.*

TWR   You said you resisted making the husband have an affair for a long time. What made you give up that resistance?

JO   Well, it was a slow deterioration in the relationship originally, but at a certain point I wanted there to be more emotional momentum. I also came across a Katherine Anne Porter quote: 'Physical infidelity is the signal, the notice given, that all fidelities might be undermined.' The *NYRB* review of *Dept.* called infidelity 'the smallest possible disaster'. And it is, in some ways, a small disaster – and in another way, it's the thing that people blow up their lives for. As for all those ideas about 'this has already been done' – well, at a certain point you realise it's madness to think that a story's been told too many times, because it's all in the execution. I wouldn't say the way I told the story was *new*, exactly, but I had a particular interest in writing a philosophical novel set in what is usually considered the domestic sphere. There's more of a tradition of that in European literature, but still there aren't many of those novels that have a female protagonist. And even if they do – think of Jean Rhys's work for example – it's often someone who is very loosely tethered to those around them, and that creates a kind of knockabout feeling. When I was in my late twenties and I was teaching at a summer school in Oxford, I would take my money when it was over, and go to the station and just pick a city on the departures board, and go there and travel around. It was scary, and it was fun... and at the time, I *was* untethered. I had a lot of time in New York too, walking and walking around the city alone. So I wanted to write a book about that, and to ask: what does it mean if you are that kind of person, but you haven't chosen that completely solo, untethered life? I decided that I would interrupt whatever mode my character was in with its opposite. So if her thoughts were floating out there, have a concrete domestic moment that would pull her back. But also the opposite, because there is a lot of time, when you're a mother, when you're waiting. It's a very strange kind of freedom and constraint. Sometimes you do have to walk and walk and walk, to try to get a baby to stop crying, but it's so different from walking alone, because you're responsible for another creature.

TWR   Do you think it's possible to be in a domestic set-up but to retain some of that loneliness, or that untethered feeling, if you need it to write?

JO   It probably depends on your temperament. You hear about some people, Grace Paley or Alice Munro, who can sit and write at the kitchen table.

There are always those people, but I'm not one of them, so I was always looking for other models. And the ones who *can* write are very irritated by the idea that you can't keep going the whole time. They find it so precious. But maybe those people are just not very depressive. They just don't tend in that direction; they tend towards making and doing. I *am* depressive, and I write very slowly. That's always been the main thing. I've been thinking about my new novel: the main character, at a certain point, after not paying very much attention to climate change, is tuning into what's going on and how much faster it's moving than expected. And I probably read thirty books for that: I read books to understand the science of it, I read books – these were ones I was much more interested in – to understand the sociology of it, the denial, what does it mean to be frightened of something invisible? I read about terror management and all sorts of things, and I swear to God, all that reading will end up being one line in the novel. And that was a lot of time! But there was a period when I didn't know much, and then I learned and learned and learned. For a while everything was shaded by it. Someone would tell me that they were going to have their kid learn Mandarin, and I would think to myself, *That's* not what you need to be teaching your kid.

TWR   You mean they should be teaching their kid how to survive a flood instead?
JO   It's more that I just don't think that the world people are imagining is the world that we'll have. One of the seeds for this book, which is now pretty buried, is Paul Kingsnorth's essay 'Confessions of a Recovering Environmentalist', where he says he's done. He's just done with environmental activism being his life. I was fascinated by the idea that somebody could be doing something for years and then just walk away from it. So I started doing my own reading, and at a certain point if you go deep enough into the research, you see the scientists talking to each other. And when they're just talking to each other, it's *so dark*. It's insanely dark. So I wanted to write a book that was in some ways similar in form to *Dept.*, but was also about: OK, you've been tending your own garden, but what if the world outside is on fire? Is anything required of you? Especially if you're someone who's already taking care of lots of people, as the main character is.

TWR   Because a lot of her family members are suffering with mental illness.
JO   She has a lot of things going on in her family, and her role is to be the caretaker. It's been interesting, but it's also been hard to take an amorphous idea like that. And I have a bad – or maybe it's not bad, maybe it's good – a thing I've often done with my books. I've often taken something I don't like: I don't like books about childhood very much, and I don't like books about marriage, or certainly not about a writer in Brooklyn – I'd be the first one to say that that's *so* tedious. And then it almost becomes a constraint to work against. I feel like it's impossible right now to be an American and not to think about politics, and what it means to be living at this time. But I also don't tend to love novels that foreground contemporary politics, because they feel dated really easily. You engage with the moment, and then the moment passes. So I'm trying to figure out a way round that. It's been difficult. I think I always want some semi-impossible constraint to go up against when I write.

TWR   So you can take the constraint and turn it into the kind of novel you would want to read?
JO   Yes, maybe. What would it look like if I *did* want to read it? In *Dept. of Speculation*, with the marriage and the affair, I was thinking: in this kind of novel, usually only a few of the characters are allowed empathy. I thought it would be interesting if the main character was porous enough that everyone received empathy. She tells her husband, after his affair, 'I'm sorry I let you get so lonely.' And I was hoping it could be funny, too. I wanted the funny and the sad at the same time. There are amazing books that are just sad, and I'm sure there are amazing books that are just funny too, but when the funny and sad are together, those are the books I love and read over and over.

TWR   When you're writing, are you aware of that? Do you think, 'I need a joke now' or 'I need something funny here'?
JO   It feels almost musical, as if I'm aware tonally we've gone really far in one direction, so either a moment that has more emotional depth is needed, or a sort of off-hand joke. Or a fragment from philosophy. I like deadpan humour, so I don't want to signal 'Here's a joke' too obviously. It's interesting when I do readings, because audiences laugh at really different things. There are super-dark jokes

in the book that go over well in London and New York, with the writer-crowds, but don't work so well elsewhere.

TWR   Are there other things in the book that get different responses?

JO   People who are not married and don't have kids often really respond to the loneliness and the depressive beginning of the book. A friend of mine read it and got to the scene where the couple aren't married yet and they're on vacation. They're in this beautiful place, and the narrator is wondering what it would be like to live there, and she thinks, *Would it fix my brain*? My friend said that line was the whole book. The main character is always asking: will it fix my brain? If I write, if I get married, if I have a child? And of course the answer is no. That's a faulty formulation of the problem. Because what I hope becomes clear later in the book is the idea that the whole range of human emotion is... I don't know if it's exactly *welcomed*, but it shouldn't be pushed away.

TWR   A fixed brain isn't the most desirable state.

JO   Right. You know, I know people with fixed brains, and sometimes they're hard to be around in their own way.

TWR   Do you think it's hard to be inside that kind of brain, too?

JO   Maybe. I'm not a very anxious person. I've recently been thinking more about that side of things. I've realised that anxious people are often very high-functioning, the do-everything-right kind of people, and I was trying to figure out the difference, what makes people go one way or another. Of course, you can't truly generalise, but my experience has been that sometimes. If nothing has really gone terribly wrong yet, they're more likely to be anxious. Possibly there's a belief that if you do things right, everything might turn out OK. And the people I know who are more on the depressive side, they haven't believed that for a long time, maybe since childhood.

TWR   Things will *not* go OK.

JO   Well... things will *go*. They won't go one way though. There's not the idea of: *we must perfect this*. There's more of a 'things fall apart' feeling. You might reassemble them but... things fall apart.

TWR   Is that a kind of resilience?

JO   Yes, I think it is a kind of resilience. But I also think there's a resilience to being a high-functioning person who can take whatever hard things are going on in their life and turn them into a tangible object that they make, or house that they clean, or dinner that they cook. There's a whole bunch of different ways that we organise our minds to look away from the fear and dread that we naturally default to. Depression, at least in my experience, can be a wallowing in how fearful and dreadful things can be. I've always been interested in how much of your temperament you're born with, and how much you can force yourself to change. So for me, it's about *not* defaulting to fear. In fact, I was really angry after Trump won, because my natural tendency is to think, *He's going to win, he's totally going to win*, and of course polls did not predict it, and cooler minds said no, it's not going to happen, and I shouldn't worry. I was *so angry* afterwards. I would have prepared for it better! I was mad at my shrink, all those times she told me not to think about the worst-case scenario. Then I went and looked at my book ordering history and I was like, *Oh right, there was some subliminal stuff going on.*

TWR   You *were* preparing for it?

JO   I had ordered all these books on WWII, and resistance, and some spycraft stuff, totally dumb stuff.

TWR   How far had you got in your new novel when Trump was elected? And how have you had to change the novel because of his election?

JO   Well, I knew a fair number of people – and I remember this happening after 9/11 too – who, whatever they were working on, suddenly after the election were asking themselves, Does this matter? But I was already working on a book that was engaging with questions of what it means to be silent, and so on. I was really fascinated by the work of the South African sociologist Stanley Cohen, who wrote a book called *States of Denial*, about looking away from atrocities. A few people had mentioned it in connection to why we can't talk about climate change, and there were a couple of details in that book that really stuck with me. During the military regime in Brazil in the 1970s, for example, when a lot of torture was happening, there was a phrase called 'innerism': lots of middle-class people looking away from the political situation and becoming particularly interested in their hobbies. And there was a way in which, when I was thinking about climate change before Trump, I would see all these people I know developing various obsessions, and it just seemed that what they were really saying was, *I'm not going to look at* that *thing*.

TWR   What kind of obsessions?
JO   Oh, you know, food, the search for the perfect this and the perfect that...it feels a little end of the Roman Empire-ish, sometimes. There's a kind of avidity about it. But then, I can't cook very well, and of course I'm saying this all from my own desk chair. I'm not really a joiner. My idea of hell is sitting in a meeting where a consensus has to be reached. It's truly just not what I want. But with climate change, I was starting to feel that more was required of me. And when Trump was elected, it was that times a thousand. Then I had a moment when I realised that if I didn't incorporate the election, the book would be frozen in amber. But trying to incorporate it led me down a very wrong road for a few months, because everything was happening so fast. I had decided I wasn't going to say Trump's name, and everything would still be approached slantwise, but the constantly changing news was hard to handle. Right now I'm trying to figure out what to do. It was going to be set before *and* after the election, and now I think the whole thing will be set after, more or less. I'm really interested in how to write about being scared, and not feeling at home with action. Sort of like in *Dept. of Speculation*, where I was asking what would happen if a depressive, solitary person was trying to be in a very enmeshed, involved domestic situation. Where would all those free-floating thoughts and feelings go? Now I'm trying to figure out how a bookish person would try to engage with this moment in time. And like all bookish people do, my librarian is looking at past ideas about what it means to collaborate or not collaborate, what does it mean to have civic courage, those kind of ideas. So that's what I've recalibrated: how much of the novel is going to be recognisable as this exact moment in time, and how much of it is going to be about the inherent instability and fragility of any society. I think it took them 200 years to realise the Roman Empire was collapsing, and all the while the rich were moving further and further out of the city. Right now there are all these super-rich tech people getting boltholes in New Zealand. I was really interested in this phenomenon, and then last year the *New Yorker* published an article about it. I was like, 'Damn it! He got it all on record; I guess I'll take it out of the book.'

TWR   So you have taken it out of the book?
JO   Sort of. It's stayed in the book in a very small form, a compressed form. Once something feels like it's out there in the world, and people are engaging with it in an art form, even if it's journalism rather than fiction, then I lose some interest in it. It's probably a character flaw.

TWR   You lose interest because you feel that it's no longer yours?
JO   Which is ridiculous, I realise. But I'm just saying... yeah, it's totally ridiculous, but it's the way I am. It happened after the election, too. Some time before that, I had gone from being a low-level lefty, not evangelical about anything, to being the person who, if you got me too drunk at a party, would be telling you about climate disasters. And then once climate change was on the front of the *New York Times Magazine*, and after the election, people started emailing me, wanting to talk more about it.

TWR   But by then you'd moved on.
JO   Well, I had stopped needing to tell people about it, because I was wrestling with how I was going to write about it. It had become an artistic question. How do I write about this in a way that isn't boring? I'm inherently super-bored by environmental things. So I told myself that if there are any environmental things that, after four or five years of thinking about them, still feel as if they have a magnetic charge – well, those can stay. Everything else has to go.

TWR   Can you give me an example of one of the things that stayed interesting?
JO   There's a comparative religion scholar whose name is Mircea Eliade, and he said that he looked at all the endtime myths of different cultures, and he couldn't find one of a slow apocalypse. He said that in a way, maybe we understand the idea of the atomic bomb, because it corresponds to some mythic structure of it all ending suddenly. I remember reading a Swiss artist Roman Signer, who said that what we think of as the apocalypse is actually a long, slow process of the world becoming increasingly uninhabitable. It's already arrived in some places, and it will spread to others. He was

talking about post-industrial, broken-down towns in Europe.

TWR   So this is not necessarily climate change. It's late capitalism too, all kinds of things.
JO   Lots of different things. And it's really hard to let go of the myth of progress. That was one of the things that was so useful to me about Black Lives Matter, because a lot of the activists were saying that progress is an illusion that you can only have if you're in a privileged position. The #MeToo movement is the same: very few women responded by saying, 'Wow, that's a surprise! Sounds like a lot of people are being creepy to women!' No woman I know felt that way. And yet there were a lot of people, well-meaning men, who *were* surprised. There are the generational questions, too. I remember realising that a story I tell as a joke, about someone being a super-creep, could actually be the worst thing that ever happened to someone else. I don't say that to devalue their experience, but it's strange. And it's tricky because the language part of me is all about distinctions and calibrations, but larger social movements are not necessarily about that. They're about which way we want to go forward.

TWR   At the beginning of the #MeToo movement, Claire Dederer wrote an essay in the *Paris Review* about how it feels to consume art made by terrible, abusive men (she was thinking about Woody Allen in particular), and she borrowed your phrase 'art monster' to think about the self-ishness that's necessary to make art. Do you think there's a connection between that selfishness and a certain kind of entitlement in other areas, too?
JO   Well, the art monster thing has been a little odd. It was just a phrase I made up, as something my character was thinking. I remember reading a *Paris Review* interview with William Faulkner, and they asked him whether he ever worried about hurting the people he was writing about, and he said, '"Ode on a Grecian Urn" is worth any number of old ladies.' And when his daughter was complaining about his drinking, he told her that no one remembers Shakespeare's children. There *were* serious art monster men, back then. But I've met a lot of really cool younger women who love the phrase. One of them had an art monster tattoo! And I like that. It feels kind of cool and punk rock to me. But sometimes it gets pulled in as an anti-mother thing, as if I were somehow saying that you're a monster if you're a mother and you create something. The other day, the writer Lauren Groff tweeted that she just wrote and then deleted 2,000 words about hating the phrase 'art monster', because it's mother-shaming. She was nice about my book, but she hates the phrase. And part of me was thinking, of course she feels that way, she's at that stage where you're trying to write and trying to be a mother to young children, and it's a struggle. But at the same time, I *do* think there's something monstrous about any kind of art-making, because it's so inward. And men have traditionally felt more able to say, 'Don't come in here unless there's blood or fire – and even then, go to your mother.' It's very hard for a lot of people, but maybe for women in particular, to do that. But I don't think 'monster' is necessarily a pejorative term. In the book there's a moment where the character is remembering the worst night of her life, after she's left her husband and is spending the night in a hotel, and she tries to pray and she says, 'Dear God, dear monster, dear God, dear monster.' In mythology, the gods are also monsters, and that's what that phrase meant. It was about a kind of ferociousness and relent-lessness. It's so hard to make anything good, so for most people, it has to be their life's work. So you ask yourself: could I make something good if I put more hours into it? And some people make that choice. I thought Claire Dederer was right to say that men get a pass if they're artistic, but women don't. When Doris Lessing won the Nobel Prize for Literature, the stories really quickly became about how she had supposedly abandoned her children. That's a plot point in a lot of male artists' biographies; it's not the *lead* point. The original idea of an art monster came to me when I was watching an Andrew Goldsworthy documentary, and he's saying all these interesting things to the camera about his art, and his wife is in the background and all his children are there and he's oblivious, he's just totally single-minded. And part of me is envious of that. But I wasn't trying to call mothers, or people who make one choice or the other, monsters. Or monstrous.

TWR   It's surprising to me that someone could read the book and think it was saying that one path or the other is the right one. Both paths have amazing moments, and both paths also seem overwhelming and transformative.
JO   Exactly. It strikes me as a useless argument about balance. It sets up this idea that we should

all just keep a steady state. But in fact, sometimes you're swinging from the ecstatic to the trivial, and sometimes you're only going to be able to do one thing. If your child is sick or something, that's almost certainly all you're going to be able to do, and then sometimes you may be deep in a project and you lose yourself in it. A lot of people – some men, and a lot of women – ask me: number one, are *you* an art monster? And number two, do *I* have to choose? I wish I had an answer for it. I always say, oh yeah, I'm an art monster from 9 to 3.30, and then I pick up my daughter. But also, when I'm trying to get further in a book, I have to go away, and I eat like a college student, and I immediately go kind of feral, because I just want to be in my head only. And I do think there's something monstrous about losing all the domestication that you've created for yourself.

TWR   Your first book, *Last Things*, was about a relationship between a mother and a child, but told from the child's perspective. There's a moment I love in *Dept. of Speculation*, when the narrator talks about a photo of her mother with her as a baby, and her mother has this expression of naked love on her face that the narrator used to find embarrassing – but now that she herself is a mother, there's a photo of her looking at her daughter in exactly the same way. You wrote *Last Things* before you had your daughter, and that bit in *Dept. of Speculation* made me wonder whether you look back at the novel differently since becoming a mother.
JO   When my editor for *Last Things* read *Dept. of Speculation*, after it was published, he said it was like watching Grace [the child-narrator of *Last Things*] grow up. And there's a way in which that's true. The two books don't match up biographically, exactly, because Grace is an only child, and I wanted the character in *Dept.* to have a sister. But their mother left when they were children, like Grace's did. And I can feel in this new book, part of what I'm examining is what would happen if the character in *Dept. of Speculation* hadn't written a book, and had had a different sort of life. What would that life look like? So yes, there's part of me that feels that it's really interesting to be on the other side of something you didn't previously understand, or something you used to see from a different perspective. The older I get, the more that things I used not to understand, or that I used to make fun of, start to make sense to me. I'm sure that in ten years I'll probably pass into the stage where I understand why old people are always talking about their health with other old people. I mean, I get it, but I'm not there yet, so I don't *really* get it.

TWR   And you'll probably be at a different stage of life with each book you're writing.
JO   Right. The most useful thing for me about questions of life versus art was reading lots of *Paris Review* interviews, when I was younger. I only read the ones of authors I really liked, and you quickly learn that people speak with immense authority about how you should conduct your writing life. But actually, you see that one person wrote every day and another went weeks without writing; one person never left their town and another person travelled all around the world. You go through one door and it means you can't go through another, or maybe you go through the other door at a different point in time. For me, that was so liberating. And then I came across the William Carlos Williams quote: 'the artist is free'. I think about that all the time. Because it's easy to forget, when you're deep into a problem you're working on. It's easy to forget that you're free, but you are. It was a super-bad idea money-wise, and career-wise, when I wrecked the book I was working on before *Dept.*. I'd been working on a more conventional novel, and it was finished, but it had a deadness to it that I couldn't fix. So I wrecked it. And that free feeling, you know... it's the biggest indicator, to me, that I'm writing something interesting. You get to feel that you're wandering without markers and that's nerve-wracking, and it's a bad feeling in some ways, but it's exciting. If you don't have that feeling, and if you're thinking about the marketplace, or what people want to read, or about your last book... that's not the point. The point is just to get to write another book. That's always what it is. And if you finish this book, you get to write another one. And then another one and another one until you die. In some ways, that's all you can wish for.

H. R.,
New York, February 2018

BARBARA KASTEN

Barbara Kasten has been making photographic works that combine painterly
and sculptural concerns since the early 1970s. Born in 1936 in Chicago, she
trained as a painter and textile artist at the University of Arizona in the 1960s.

Working with common, industrial materials and forms, her early photograms
were made by exposing light-sensitive paper to arrangements of window screening
and plexiglass boxes. The result – as seen in the 'Photogenic Paintings' series
[1974–6] – is a kind of visual collage which Kasten calls 'spatial pastiche'.

In 1979, Kasten moved away from the camera-less technique of the photogram
and began photographing sculptural installations constructed specifically for the
lens. Lit by hot-lights – used on film sets and for studio photography – the
assemblages were rearranged and repurposed after each shoot.

For the series 'Metaphase' (1986) she built large-scale sets out of mirror,
Plexiglass, wire, corrugated plastic, and cones. The resulting images are almost
pure photographic abstraction: mesmeric coils of electric blue, dusty pinks, and
orange triangles, a distinctly 1980s colour palette in keeping with the aesthetic
of Memphis New Design.

In the decades since, Kasten's method has continued to evolve. In the series
'Studio Constructs' (2007) and 'Scene' (2012), she photographed the effects of
light and shadow produced by intersecting sheets of Plexiglass, in muted silvery
monochromatic tones. Where earlier works echo artists and designers including
Bauhaus, Moholy-Nagy, and Constructivism, the sculpting of light in these later
works is akin to artists such as James Turrell.

PLATES

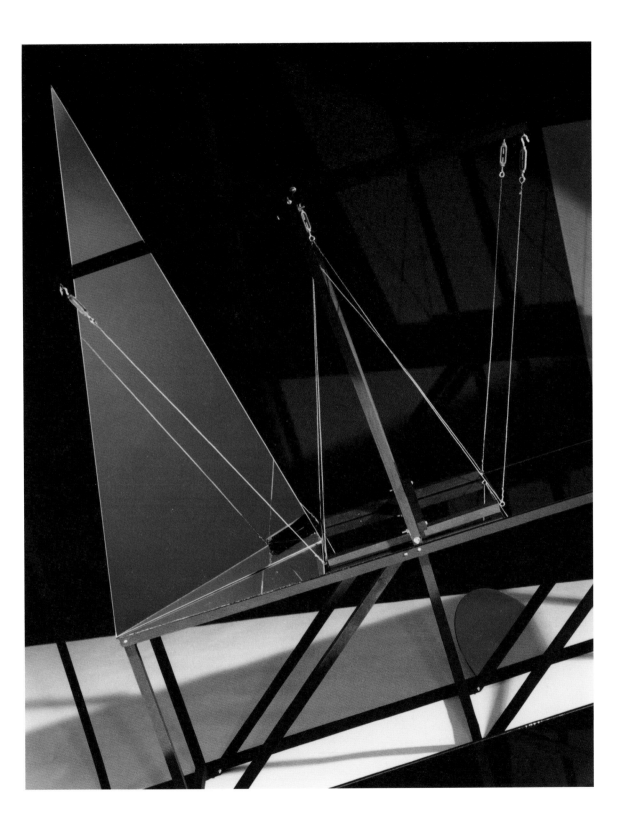

SOME HEAT: READING AND WRITING WOMEN INTO AND OUT OF THE FIRE

QUINN LATIMER

I spend my days in the desert reading about women on fire. Ingeborg Bachmann, Toni Morrison's Hannah Peace, Fleur Jaeggy's Fraulein von Oelix, Bhanu Kapil's Ban. In the newspapers, female gymnasts, journalists, actresses, prisoners, curators, soldiers, professors and students, indigenous and environmental activists – and their fellow women who watch it all. Watch what? The flames licking at their mothers, their elders, their sisters, their daughters, their strangers. To get away from such reports, literary or literal, *their fires*, I walk. The blonde, brittle fields I move across in the afternoons, jumping the ranch fence of my borrowed house in the desert, are pale as though on fire, or once on fire. I think about my mother as I walk them and the brushfires that burned all the way to the Pacific, jumping the highway, in the days after she died. I think about fire. As nature or its metaphor. As violence or its metaphor. As culture – all of its metaphors. In this arid landscape, so much kindling, I think about the wildfires burning, always annually but with increasing intensity, in California, Greece, Portugal, Italy, Texas, Alberta. Anywhere there is fuel. I think about the fires of women. I take their temperature. A world of women watching (then narrating) women burn. The way we are taught to expect then examine the heat.

As I write this, I am staying in another woman's house, reading from her extensive library. I read Toni Morrison's novel *Sula*, with its virtuosic, flame-filled female friendships and matrilineal orders, and the violence enacted upon them, set in a poor African-American hamlet high in the lush hills of Ohio paradoxically called The Bottom. I read Swiss writer Fleur Jaeggy's caustic short stories describing moneyed and idiosyncratic Mitteleuropean women in the Alps, and their accidental or chosen families, including Jaeggy's own close friendship with the celebrated Austrian poet and writer Ingeborg Bachmann. In one small autofiction, Jaeggy discreetly delineates Bachmann's subtle, burning life and her fiery death (smoking in bed, they said, unsure if the fire was deliberate – suicide – or an accident). 'Every day I went to Sant'Eugenio, the burn unit,' Jaeggy writes, of visiting Bachmann in Rome as she died. 'Twice I entered a room that had to be kept aseptic.'

I read Morrison's and Jaeggy's careful words in a place of little rain and the potential for much burning. The radical and radically disparate worlds they conjure are separated by geography, economy, and racism, but they are unalterably connected by gender and the women that burn at their centre. By a strange sisterhood of fire and womanhood. As I look around at the desert that surrounds me, at the books that enclose me, this literary sisterhood seems familiar, despite its distances. Indeed, in this place, a mostly empty, high desert region just north of the US-Mexican border, every book I pick up features a scene of a woman burning, and other women watching or setting that fire. I must be clear: I am not looking for these literary scenes; this is not a specific research project I have come here to embark on. I have come to the desert to relax after an exhausting professional project. For the first time in a couple of years I am reading only for pleasure – whatever that means – and yet each novel or book of poetry or theory I pull from the long, stacked bookshelves in this sprawling ranch house where I am staying singes my fingers. A woman is burning in it.

In this desert, I do not only read and walk, noting the fires currently or historically burning. I also find myself compulsively taking baths, as if to cool the flames that might engulf me. Sinking into the depths of my large, borrowed tub, which is large enough to accommodate my entire, outstretched body, I read from the English-born, Colorado-based poet

Bhanu Kapil's *Ban en Banlieue*. Despite the book's dampness, its relative 'English' wetness, it seems related to my current indiscriminate research. Kapil's *Ban* is a book-length poem that 'traces an outline around the charred remains of those disposable [female] bodies', bodies and bodies of work like that of the artist Ana Mendieta and writer Theresa Hak Kyung Cha, and Nirbhaya, the young student who was raped and disemboweled on a New Delhi bus, then left to die in the street. In one section of the book, titled 'Embryology for Ban', Kapil writes:

> The image that precedes Ban is the strangely intrusive image of a drowned woman. At the last moment, she escapes her husband's pyre, contorting or lifting her body into the river. She leaps into the river, fully clothed, her body on fire. That rapid cooling creates a bronze figure. River dolphins carry her to the Bay of Bengal, where microscopic sea creatures nibble away at the burns.

This image of the 'rapid cooling that creates a bronze figure' rhymes in my head with a scene from Morrison's *Sula*, in which Hannah Peace's dress catches on fire as her mother and daughter watch:

> Mr and Mrs Suggs, who had set up their canning apparatus in their front yard, saw her running, dancing toward them. They whispered, 'Jesus, Jesus,' and together hoisted up their tub of water in which tight red tomatoes floated and threw it on the smoke-and-flame-bound woman. The water did put out the flames, but it also made steam, which seared to sealing all that was left of the beautiful Hannah Peace. She lay there on the wooden sidewalk planks, twitching lightly among the smashed tomatoes, her face a mask of agony so intense that for years the people who gathered round would shake their heads at the recollection of it.

Hannah's mother Eva, one-legged, in her room upstairs, throws herself out the window to try to vanquish the flames engulfing her daughter in the yard below, but falls too short on the ground to do anything but cry out. Conversely, outside Hannah's daughter Sula stands to the side, unmoving, as though transfixed or simply 'interested', as Eva recalls later. She does not attempt to save her mother.

Likewise, another rhyming image of another daughter, or a kind of daughter, watching her elder burn, from my recent reading: in Jaeggy's short story 'The Heir', the servant girl Hannelore watches with glee, perhaps, or simple (never so simple) interest, as her benefactor, Fraulein von Oelix, goes up in flames:

> 'Are you warm, Madam?' Hannelore asked. The gaze triumphant and mean. The flames were roasting the fraulein like a sacrificial animal. She was not unlike one on a spit. The fraulein felt no pain. While the flames enveloped her she felt a terrible longing. For what she didn't have. For what she'd never had. She did not fear death. The longing – or perhaps the despair over all the nothing – was so acute as to make death seem mild to her. Her hands, like the claws of a crustacean, clutched a little mound of dust.

To say that life itself, in its current iteration, strewn with and striated by violence – including the violence inflicted on and by language – is like clutching a little mound of dust, does not seem hyperbolic. Not here, fires all around. I read these books, I read the newspapers, I live in the world, with its expert and seemingly indestructible misogyny, I walk this desert, and I try to name the violence, to be pointed and plain: gender violence, environmental violence, the violence of racism and poverty twisting through both, the violence of patriarchy and empire, and capital, the scaffolding of all, the very furnace, the fuel. But it is not enough. These pat definitions, their expected qualifiers and more evocative metaphors, do not conjure the reality of all the burning expected of us, as spectator or victim. I wonder about Hannelore, though. And Sula. Their strangely dutiful watching – enigmatic or no, gleeful or no – as their mothers caught fire. In a world in which women burn regularly, are taught to expect 'some heat', other women watch. I watch.

If reading is itself a kind of watching, a kind of literary voyeurism, it is never more so than when reading depictions of violence. This voyeurism is amplified when the texts are not novels, not stories, but newspaper accounts of violence: detailed records of the real. And lately those media reports are more often than not about violence against women – even more than usual for what is a reliably 'hot' topic. It is a story that has no bottom. Is it ironic that violence against women is regarded as a women's issue – as though the fires of misogyny were self-immolations, no men present or involved at all – and is thus a constant subject not simply for the newspapers but for the specific media that courts a female readership? This means, then, that everything I read in print or online – from the national newspapers to political journals to fashion magazines to blogs about wellness and beauty – teems with detailed narratives of the destruction of women. And I read them. Every single article. And after each reading a question appears above me like smoke: What does it do to the woman reader and writer to incessantly read such reports? To watch, in other words, the violence repeatedly enacted against bodies like my own? 'Seeing was writing', the German painter and critic Jutta Koether wrote in her feminist novella *f*. And indeed it can feel as though by reading these daily accounts of gendered violence that I am writing them myself. My reading-*cum*-watching-*cum*-writing feels like a distinct and shameful kind of voyeurism; I feel complicit. Or at least entangled to an extent that is difficult to understand. I cannot explain away the sense of shame that such stories leave me with; it is simply there, a brutal fact casting its shadow of humiliation over every pale page.

I think about the recently reignited feminist movements – MeToo, among them – and the flames of women flickering around every page I read. Each voice raised, body or land violated, another log on the fire. Another house (of patriarchy, its slow- and fast-burning violence) burned – but not quite down. What kind of houses? Every kind, from film production houses to the White House. All momentarily on fire – lit by the violence of the men who reside in them, lit by the suddenly visible flames of women who burn in them, narrated in the papers, on the news – and then extinguished. The extinguishing water being one man fired, or one man's weak apology. Some smoke. Ashes. Nothing more to see here. There is a term for this in the language of fire: controlled burns. A fire lit and managed to reduce the intensity and magnitude of bigger wildfires by depleting that which is flammable, that which is fuel. These fires, then, are not the destruction of the patriarchal system but a way to protect it. A line I remember from a newspaper article years ago, reported during a brushfire in California, echoes across my mind, its singed landscape: 'Let it burn. Get rid of the fuel.' A local woman's voice saying this, of course. The reporter getting it down, on paper. Another flammable.

To burn with shame – a phrase that seems reliably feminine, even if there is no grammatical gender indicated as such (in English). As women we all know it, though. It's how violence – particularly patriarchal violence – operates. In order for the perpetrator to remain untouched, he must ignite shame in his victim; a shame that by definition burns only her. Women are taught to be good at this: shame and its self-sacrifice. Women are taught to take the heat. But there are different kinds of fires. Sometimes that singular and singularly feminine shame – sparked and spoken out loud – begins to catch and spread. It turns away from the self and becomes something collective, a kind of chorus, until finally: solidarity. One woman's voice ignites another, and another, and another. Recently, I've been reading such fires – they are called accusations but most women readers know them, shamefully, as truths – in the newspapers nearly every day. The controlled burns that follow are lit by men as they dismiss the worst (or simply the most expendable) offenders, then announce heroically that the fire has been put out, leaving the existing patriarchal system in place. At every level, in each institution, in every field.

And yet: 'Fire is fire', a Ventura woman is quoted as saying in a newspaper late last year, during the terrible wildfires in California, the worst in its recorded history. Fire is also itself – no metaphor of destruction, no woman at its centre. This observation, 'Fire is fire', also reminds me of a line from an article a decade ago that has stayed with me, as echo or prophecy: 'California has two seasons: fire and flood.' From Europe this past autumn, I combed the US newspapers online for images of the Southern California towns where I grew up, their sober captions aflame. 'The remains of the Vista del Mar hospital after the Thomas wildfire swept through Ventura', one photo caption reads. The image it accompanies reveals the psychiatric hospital, where I'd visit my mother as a child, to be a burned remnant of collapsed frames, a line of skinny palm trees and an ashy horizon of foothills behind. Another newspaper image – an even, apocalyptic orange – shows smoke from the Thomas fire as it crossed over Lake Casitas near Ojai. My mother's ashes are there. Or were. There were brushfires burning a decade ago, when we placed them there.

I look outside the window of the house I am staying in: dry prairie for as far as I can see. Brittle yellow grasslands. Some white-blue sky like a sign for flood or its reticence above it. The fire season is over, I calculate, or is it? In some states in the country I am currently in, fire's sister, flood, has come. Not here, though. The landscape outside my window is resolutely dry. Nevertheless, I ask myself one more question: Why do I keep coupling the ever-burning fires of misogyny whose smoke is suddenly being seen and acknowledged across our media with the actual fires spiraling out across our natural environments and cities, spurred on by the patriarchal ecocide in which our natural world is being deformed? Why do I keep looking to the arid desert – so much tinder – that surrounds me, engulfs me, for an answer? Why this constant coupling in my mind of culture and nature?

Another image, another charred bit of language I found and read on the edge of the desert, asserts itself, catches a kind of fire in my mind:

> Images exist, and the causes of, reasons for the images. Sometimes I believe there are no causes or reasons. Or no images, just the causes: fire, earth, air, water. These four also might be images and hidden, another reason or cause, an endless, unknown infinity.

Kathy Acker ends this passage, from her first novel *The Childlike Life of the Black Tarantula by the Black Tarantula*, with the (possibly appropriated) line: 'I am an old man talking.' I'm not sure about that but I get the humour, the need for some quiet drag. I get the causes, the images, the fire – also earth, air, water. That which surrounds us, douses us, enflames us and others. Causes, though: we keep looking for them. Why? Fire is an element, yes, but it is also an image. Wet and dry. Why, though, is female pain, the destruction of the female body, and the male violence that causes it, treated as elements as well, parts of the 'natural order' we must become 'naturalised' to? In this world we have inherited or taken (mostly taken with an inherited violence, let's be honest), we swim through female destruction like water; we observe it like fire. It is the earth we walk, and the air we breathe. These are not hidden images, nor are they elements. They are something else.

'You were on fire,' David Streitfeld says to Ursula K. Le Guin in an interview from last November, before she passed away this January. He was talking about her literary production of the late 1960s and early 70s, when she wrote *The Left Hand of Darkness* and *The Dispossessed*, and began the first of her *Earthsea* novels. She is frankly unimpressed by his metaphor – her scepticism rises like smoke off the page – but it makes me think about Le Guin's farsighted coupling in her work of feminism and environmentalism: the tight knot of gender and racial difference, resource exploitation and land appropriation, that she unravelled again and again. 'For thirty years I've been saying, we are making the world uninhabitable, for God's sake,' she famously said. In her novels, stories, poetry and essays, the fires of femicide and ecocide originate from the same source, an inexhaustible patriarchy – the fixed fuel of our damaged and damaging societies – that would burn us all down, then disavow the smoke.

Traditional dystopian works of art often depict apocalypse as images of nuclear-made distortion, lands of ash-filled abjection. But perhaps the present fires whose facts fill our days and eyes, our newspapers and monitors, those fires of 'nature' – man-made, as always – are the warning images of apocalypse, the smoke not to be ignored. We should not only watch the earth as it burns, we should listen to what it is telling us. And we should heed the the women who try to protect it. Last year, in 2017, nearly 200 indigenous environmental activists – many of them women working to protect land and natural resources across the world, in Brazil, Honduras, the Philippines, Cambodia, Mexico and elsewhere – were murdered in physical and systemic violence enabled by international corporations and the corrupt regimes that support them. The violence these women were met with as they defended their forests and water came from men and their industry: mining, agribusiness, logging, dams, poaching. They include celebrated activists like Honduran indigenous leader, Berta Cáceres, whose recent unsolved murder is linked to her campaign against the internationally financed Agua Zarca hydroelectric dam. It is said that 80 per cent of the earth's biodiversity remains on indigenous lands – those women who endeavour to protect them from private and state exploitation (often one and the same in neoliberal governance) are increasingly vulnerable to violence. Meanwhile, the annual brushfires that I grew up with in California have become increasingly catastrophic. A stark symbol of our current dystopia and its relentless carceral state is that many of the people fighting those fires in California are the state's women prisoners.

In a recent article in the *New York Times Magazine* on 'The Incarcerated Women Who Fight California's Wildfires', writer Jaime Lowe describes the lives of the 250 or so women prisoners who work as state firefighters for less than two dollars an hour. (Male prisoners are also used as firefighters, but in separate units.) Most of these women are in prison for drug- or alcohol-related offences that in a less draconian society would not warrant imprisonment at all; some, like 22-year-old Shawna Lynn Jones, die fighting California's fires nominally for free. Before being placed as firefighters, the women prisoners are given three weeks of training compared to the three-year apprenticeship that 'free' firefighters receive. Such dangerous prison labour conjures up images of black men imprisoned in American mines and lumber camps after Reconstruction – the work of the 13th Amendment's clause that allowed 'involuntary servitude' (slavery) to continue as punishment for 'crime'. Consider the Black Codes, a series of state laws enacted after the American Civil War and Reconstruction that criminalised petty offences with the aim of keeping freed Black people tied to their former owners' plantations and farms through 'convict labour'. The resulting convict lease system in the United States mostly leased out its prisoners to industries of natural resource exploitation – minerals, timber – undertaken on indigenous lands expropriated from Native Americans. California's inmate firefighters invoke images of America's ubiquitous chain gangs. Indeed, Lowe notes that when they're at work the female inmate firefighters in California 'look like chain gangs without the chains, especially when out working in Malibu, where the average annual household income is 238,000 dollars.' One of the inmate firefighters, a woman named La'Sonya Edwards, says: 'There are some days we are worn down to the core ... this isn't that different from slave conditions.'

As climate change progresses while profiteers and politicians deny its existence, drought and the resulting wildfires worsen each year. As such the inmate firefighters are increasingly called on; they are conceived to be a 'state resource' that saves California taxpayers around 100 million dollars a year. Lowe writes, 'In the fall of 2014, as the state's courts were taking up the issue of overcrowded prisons, the office of California's attorney general argued against shrinking the number of inmates. Doing so, it claimed, "would severely impact fire camp participation, a dangerous outcome while California is in the middle of a difficult fire season and severe drought." The logic? Climate change necessitates that we imprison more people, then use them to protect our cities. It's as dark as it sounds; the statistics singe. According to a 2014 report by the International Centre for Prison Studies, nearly a third of all female prisoners in the world are incarcerated in the US. The American prison industrial complex is an industry that's 'on fire', one might say.

Over the span of nearly my entire life, from 1980 to 2014, the rate of growth for female imprisonment in the US has outpaced men by more than 50 per cent. As I walk across a field of potential tinder, its pale glitter, I imagine a speculative growth chart: as each year passes, more women are locked away, then let out, only to be placed at the bottom of a wall of fire.

In arid Athens late last year, many months after its own capacious fire season, when flames darkened the mountains that ring the city, I saw Angela Davis speak on carceral capitalism, an economic and ideological system that depends on the prison state. Her answer? An abolitionist feminism. Feminism, moreover, as a methodology of struggle. A methodology that goes beyond genre, to study issues that initially do not seem to focus on gender, be they war, imperialism, incarceration, environmentalism or land rights. She argued that we should consider feminism the very ground (and air and water) from which we are attempting a radical transformation of the structures, institutions and relationships that define and loop through our lives. In one of her jailhouse interviews given from a California state prison in the early 1970s, Davis recalled, 'My earliest childhood memories are bound up with the sounds of dynamite.' These fire bombings of black homes and churches in her neighbourhood of Birmingham, Alabama, included the church bombing that killed four small girls who were friends of Davis's, and students of her mother. Speaking from jail, she notes: 'Certainly you can't separate the movement inside the prisons from the black liberation movement which has been evolving over years and years and years.'

In my present desert, where I read and walk and imagine disparate feminisms amid our carceral states, prisons constellating the distances, the land is fanned by expanses of dry yellow grasses broken only by alien green agave, raised hands of dark mesquite, and ranch fence. I imagine that the gold of the grasses have always been gilded this way, but I am told that when the cattle ranchers of the American settler society took these lands more than a century ago from their Native inhabitants, the land was greener – there was more, potentially, for the ranchers' animals to eat. Violence – both environmental and genocidal – has turned this land to the pale patina I know it by today. The town where I'm staying was estab-lished more than a century ago as a water stop on the railroad used for western colonial expansion after the Mexican War of 1848; military forts nearby were used to fight and slaughter the Native Americans and then Mexicans whose land this originally was. During the Civil War, when nearby Fort Davis was briefly abandoned for fighting in the East, I read that 'Indians used the wood from its buildings for fuel.'

Fuel comes in so many forms, though. As the Palestinian poet and statesman Mahmoud Darwish wrote famously in his poem 'To the Reader': 'Black irises in my heart / and on my lips ... flame. / My fate is my anger / and all fire starts out in anger.' Does fire, as fate, always have to begin in anger? What about acquiescence? Fire can also become routine, metabolised into one's life and work (though perhaps anger is metabolic too). Consider the British poet Sophie Collins's recent untitled poem:

> The village is always on fire.
> Men stay away from the kitchens,
> take up in outhouses with concrete floors,
> while the women – soot in their hair –
> initiate the flames into their small routines.

The village is always on fire – no doubt. But why this expected female initiation of flames into our (small) routines? Why, that is, do we bring that burning into our work, whether that work is the making of literature or not? It is not enough to say that women are writing the world as it is. Such scenes, coupled with the constant and daily newspaper accounts of sexual harassment and violence that I read on my glowing screens, raise for me the more general question: Why are women on fire such insistent and incandescent images, both literary and literal? How am I to under-stand this incessant burning of women in fiction, particularly as written by women writers?

I think suddenly of Virginia Woolf's Angel in the House, that charm-ing, self-sacrificing, ever-deadening and inescapable feminine figure who lives to serve man and family, and who the writer describes in her devas-tating lecture 'Professions for Women'. And describes killing. 'Killing the Angel in the House was part of the occupation of a woman writer,' Woolf

writes, without pause. I think too of Deborah Levy's recent memoir of
her divorce and the writing that came after, in which she quotes a letter
from Simone De Beauvoir to Nelsen Algren. In it, De Beauvoir writes: 'I
want everything from life, I want to be a woman and to be a man, to have
many friends and have loneliness, to work much and write good books.'
Compelled by that wish of De Beauvoir's, to be both woman and man,
Levy writes:

> [I]t was obvious to me that femininity, as written by men and per-
> formed by women, was the exhausted phantom that still haunted
> the early twenty-first century. There were not that many women
> I knew who wanted to put the phantom together again. She is a
> very tricky character to play and it is a role (sacrifice, endurance,
> cheerful suffering) that has made some women go mad. This was
> not a story I wanted to hear all over again. It was time to find other
> main female characters with other talents.

I read fire in those lines of Levy's: behind them I see women burning.
Woolf's Angel, Levy's 'exhausted phantom', Collins's women with soot in
their hair, Kapil's widow twisting away from her husband's funeral pyre,
Morrison's Hannah Peace, so many others. These figures, as Woolf writes
it, need to die. Why, though? So their daughters can become writers,
so women can become professionals, so we can become human, so we
can transform and write our own lives, so we don't end up drowning in
misogyny instead? But must we continue to perform this death, over
and over, in our literature? Woolf writes that this phantom 'died hard'.
'Though I flatter myself that I killed her in the end, the struggle was
severe... But it was a real experience; it was an experience that was bound
to befall all women writers at that time. But to continue my story. The
Angel was dead; what then remained?'

Embers, but what else? When the patriarchal phantom of 'womanhood' burns, what remains? Are the women burning in the books of
Morrison, Kapil, Jaeggy, Collins, Levy and so many others such phantoms, angels of the house? To become a woman writer does one need to
set such fires? Perhaps the fires we watch or start in our literature are not
about complicity – they are about anger. ('My fate is my anger / and all
fire starts out in anger.') They are about agency, too, and necessity. Audre
Lorde's famous quote comes to me: 'I am going to write fire until it comes
out of my ears, my eyes, my noseholes – everywhere. Until it's every
breath I breathe. I'm going to go out like a fucking meteor!'

But why then do I still feel such shame when I read these literary fires,
virtuosic as they are, as though my very reading is a failure of solidarity
(and thus of imagination) with those who are being burned? I think
of Sula watching her mother burn. I think of Hannelore. Both young,
impoverished women that resolutely reject the tight and suffocating cos-
tume of womanhood and class expected of them. Their rejection takes the
form of a strange kind of movement and freedom: watching their angels
of the house burn, and being complicit in it. Their freedom is configured
as Sula's mother, the selfless, ever-available Hannah, twitching in the
dirt; as Hannelore's generous benefactor, Fraulein von Oelix, ending up
a pile of dust. Elsewhere, Toni Morrison has written that 'The function
of freedom is to free someone else.' Are these fires really setting the
women burned free? Perhaps, but not only.

I know that part of my uneasiness with such literary scenes stems
from my sense that women writers – by writing and setting these fires –

are somehow contributing to the eroticisation of their (and our) own destruction. Fire is a trope; it is glorious on the page. But even as I am drawn to its warmth, the beauty of its damage feels damaging. Perhaps this is because I identify just as much with the burning female elders as with their radical daughters. Each is a part of our self; some, like Woolf, like Morrison, are braver in its burning off. And this is likely the writers' intent. If part of violence's work is to create the feeling of complicity in its victim, the immolations of misogyny might be understood – simply, drily, ironically, tragically – as self-immolations. Or perhaps we just want to burn it all down, including ourselves.

Regardless, I wonder when such recurrent baths of fire – a burning constituted by both real and metaphoric violence, personal and state violence, economic and environmental violence, by violence internalised and violence made into literature, and by literature written, as is so often the case, out of it – won't need to be anticipated by us, attended to by us, narrated by us, reported on by us, read by us, inflicted on us. When these male pyres on which we are expected to burn will finally go out. When we won't have to take part, as spectator or participant. That's both a metaphor and not. It's the image in between, I mean.

CONTRIBUTORS

CHLOE ARIDJIS is a Mexican writer living in London. Her debut novel *Book of Clouds* was awarded the Prix du Premier Roman Etranger in France and her second novel, *Asunder*, is set in London's National Gallery. She has been involved in various art projects and was a guest curator at Tate Liverpool. In 2014 she received a Guggenheim Fellowship. Her third novel, *Sea Monsters*, comes out in February 2019.

MATTHEW BEAUMONT is a Professor of English at UCL, and the author and editor of several books, most recently *Nightwalking: A Nocturnal History of London* (Verso, 2015). He is a Co-Director of UCL's Urban Lab.

ALEX BELL lives and works in London. Her poems have appeared in magazines and journals including *The Rialto, Magma, The Quietus, Poetry Wales* and *Long Poem Magazine*. Her pamphlet *Bad Luck Woman* was published by Eyewear in 2016. She co-hosts a series of poetry and karaoke nights, and co-edited the pamphlet *Cold Fire: Poetry Inspired by David Bowie* for *The Rialto* in 2017. She is a 2017-18 TOAST Poetry mentee.

JULIA BELL is a writer of novels, poems, essays and screenplays, and Course Director of the MA Creative Writing at Birkbeck. She divides her time between London and Berlin.

ANDREA BÜTTNER creates connections between art history and social issues, and is interested in notions of poverty, shame, vulnerability, and the belief systems that underpin them. Recent solo exhibitions include Kunsthalle Wien, Vienna (2016); and Hammer Art Museum, Los Angeles (2017). She participated in the São Paulo Biennale (2010), dOCUMENTA 13 (2012), and British Art Show 8 (2015-17).

VAHNI CAPILDEO's sixth book is *Venus as a Bear* (Poetry Book Society Summer Choice 2018 and shortlisted for the 2018 Forward Prize). Capildeo's non-fiction ranges from a regular poetry report for *PN Review* to research on cocoa growing for *adda*, Commonwealth Writers' online journal. Current projects are an intersemiotic collaboration with Chris McCabe, and writing satirical character monologues for performance in traditional masquerade. Capildeo is the Douglas Caster Cultural Fellow in Poetry at the University of Leeds.

HELEN CHARMAN is writing a PhD on maternity, sacrifice and political economy in late nineteenth-century fiction at the University of Cambridge. She teaches undergraduates in Cambridge and primary school children in Hackney. She was shortlisted for the inaugural White Review Poet's Prize, and her work can be found in Carcanet's *New Poetries VII* (April 2018). Her first pamphlet, *Support, support,* is coming out with Offord Road Books in August 2018.

VERA GIACONI was born in Montevideo, Uruguay, but has lived her whole life in Buenos Aires. Her first book of short stories, *Carne Viva* (Raw Flesh), was published in 2011 by Eterna Cadencia in Argentina, and was translated into Hebrew in 2013. *Seres Queridos* (Loved Ones), her second story collection, was one of five finalists for the International Ribera del Duero Short Fiction Prize in 2015. The book was published by Anagrama in April 2017. Her stories have been published in a variety of anthologies, magazines and online publications. For over fourteen years she has worked as editor, proofreader and freelance journalist for various magazines and newspapers in Argentina, and she also teaches writing workshops.

ANNIE GODFREY LARMON is a writer and editor based in New York. She is a regular contributor to *Artforum*, and her writing has appeared in *apricota, Bookforum, CURA., Even, Frieze, MAY, Spike, Texte zur Kunst, Topical Cream, Vdrome* and *WdW Review*, among other publications. The recipient of a 2016 Creative Capital | Warhol Foundation Arts Writers Grant for short-form writing, she is the editor of publications for the inaugural Okayama Art Summit and a former international reviews editor of *Artforum*. In 2018, she was a writer in residence at the LUMA Foundation in Arles, France and at Mahler & LeWitt Studios in Spoleto, Italy. She is currently at work on her first novel.

MARIA HUMMER has lived and worked in Seoul, St. Louis, Budapest and Bratislava, and she is currently based in London. Her short stories have appeared in *Wasafiri, Best of Ohio Short Stories, Passages North*, and more. She is the writer of prize-winning short films 'He Took His Skin Off For Me' and 'Dinner and a Movie'. Her most recent film, based on her short story 'The Director', is currently in post-production with director

Kim Albright. She is a 2014 alumnus of the Writers' Centre Norwich Escalator scheme and is currently writing her first novel, a speculative fiction love story.

BARBARA KASTEN was born in 1936 in Chicago, Illinois, where she currently lives and works. She received her BFA from the University of Arizona and her MFA from the California College of Arts and Crafts. Kasten was the subject of a retrospective at the Institute of Contemporary Art in Philadelphia that travelled to the Graham Foundation in Chicago and the Los Angeles Museum of Contemporary Art. Her work is featured in the collections of the Museum of Modern Art in New York, the Tate Modern in London, The Whitney Museum of American Art and the Guggenheim Museum in New York, The Centre Pompidou, and the Smithsonian American Art Museum in Washington, DC. among many others.

QUINN LATIMER is a poet and critic whose work often explores feminist economies of writing, reading, and image production. Her books include *Like a Woman: Essays, Readings, Poems* (2017); *Sarah Lucas: Describe This Distance* (2013); *Film as a Form of Writing: Quinn Latimer Talks to Akram Zaatari* (2013); and *Rumored Animals* (2012). A frequent contributor to *Artforum* and a contributing editor of *frieze*, Latimer was editor-in-chief of publications for documenta 14 in Athens and Kassel.

MELANIE MAUTHNER's translation of Scholastique Mukasonga's novel *Our Lady of the Nile* was shortlisted for the 2016 International Dublin Literary Award.

JOHN MCCULLOUGH's first collection of poems, *The Frost Fairs* (Salt, 2011) won the Polari First Book Prize and was a Book of the Year for *The Independent* and a summer read in *The Observer*. His second, *Spacecraft* (Penned in the Margins, 2016) was named one of *The Guardian*'s Best Books for Summer and was shortlisted for the Ledbury-Forte prize. He lives in Hove.

MEGAN MCDOWELL has translated many contemporary authors from Latin America and Spain, including Alejandro Zambra, Samanta Schweblin, Mariana Enriquez, Gonzalo Torné, Lina Meruane, Diego Zuñiga and Carlos Fonseca. Her translations have been published in *The New Yorker, Tin House, The Paris Review, Harper's, McSweeney's, Words Without Borders* and *Vice*, among others. Her translation of Alejandro Zambra's novel *Ways of Going Home* won the 2013 English PEN award for writing in translation, and her English version of *Fever Dream*, by Samanta Schweblin, was shortlisted for the 2017 Man Booker International Prize. She lives in Santiago, Chile.

LUCY MERCER's poems have been published in *Poetry Review* and *Poetry London* amongst others. She is studying for a PhD in 'Speculative Emblematics'. This series is the winner of the White Review Poet's Prize 2017.

SCHOLASTIQUE MUKASONGA was born in Rwanda. She settled in France in 1992, two years before the brutal genocide of the Tutsi swept through Rwanda, after which she learned that twenty-seven members of her family were massacred. Gallimard published her autobiographical account *Inyenzi ou les Cafards* (published in English as *Cockroaches*) in 2004, followed by *La femme aux pieds bus* (Barefoot Woman) in 2008. Her first novel, *Notre-Dame du Nil*, won the Ahamadou Kourouma Prize and the Renaudot Prize in 2012, as well as the Océans France Ô Prize in 2013. Her second novel *Coeur Tambour* appeared in 2016. 'La Rivière Rukarara' was first published in *Ce que murmurent les collines: Nouvelles rwandaises* by Gallimard in 2014.

SANDEEP PARMAR is a poet, critic and Professor of English Literature at the University of Liverpool where she co-directs Liverpool's Centre for New and International Writing.

HANNAH ROSEFIELD is a contributing editor to *The White Review* and a PhD candidate in English at Harvard University, where she is writing a thesis on Victorian stepmothers. Her work has appeared in *The New Statesman, The Point, The New Republic* and *The New Yorker* online.

WASEEM YAQOOB is a lecturer in the history of political thought at the University of Cambridge, and Branch Secretary of Cambridge UCU.

PLATES

READING LIST

ON UNIVERSITIES

Ahmed, Sara, 'Complaint', *Sara N. Ahmed*. ‹www.saranahmed.com/complaint/›
   'Complaint as Diversity Work', *feministkilljoys*, 10 November 2017
   ‹https://feministkilljoys.com/2017/11/10/complaint-as-diversity-work/›
   On Being Included: Racism and Diversity in Institutional Life (Durham, NC: Duke University Press, 2012).
   Audit Cultures: Anthropological Studies in Accountability, Ethics and the Academy, ed. by Marilyn Strathern
   (Oxford: Routledge, 2001).
Campsie, Alex, 'Spectacle, spaces and political change: reflections then and now'. In *Renewal: A Journal of Social Democracy*
   [online] ‹http://www.renewal.org.uk/blog/spectacle-spaces-and-political-change›
Collini, Stefan, *Speaking of Universities* (London: Verso, 2018).
   What Are Universities For? (London: Penguin, 2012).
Freedman, Des, 'Universities ending the strikes is not a climbdown – the fight goes on', *Guardian*, 16 April 2018
   ‹https://www.theguardian.com/commentisfree/2018/apr/16/university-pensions-strikes-union-campaign›
Jones, Sophie A. and Catherine Oakley, 'The Precarious Postdoc: Interdisciplinary Research and Casualised Labour in
   the Humanities and Social Sciences', *Working Knowledge* (2018) ‹http://www.workingknowledgeps.com/wp-content/
   uploads/2018/04/WKPS_PrecariousPostdoc_PDF_Interactive.pdf›
Leathwood, Carole and Barbara Read, *Gender and the Changing Face of Higher Education: A Feminized Future?*
   (Berkshire: Open University Press, 2009).
Marris, Claire, 'Why USS pension cuts will not be spread equally', *Medium*, 3 April 2018
   ‹https://medium.com/ussbriefs/why-uss-pension-cuts-will-not-be-spread-equally-ffd323747b59›
McGettigan, Andrew, *The Great University Gamble: Money, Markets and the Future of Higher Education*
   (London: Pluto Press, 2013).
Rustin, Michael, 'The Neoliberal University and its Alternatives', *Soundings* 63 (2016), pp. 147-170
   ‹https://www.lwbooks.co.uk/sites/default/files/s63_14rustin_o.pdf›
'USSbriefs', *Medium* ‹https://medium.com/ussbriefs›

The Years by Annie Ernaux
(tr. Alison L. Strayer) is
published by Fitzcarraldo
Editions on 20 June 2018.

'One of the best books
you'll ever read.'
— Deborah Levy, author
of *Hot Milk*

Fitzcarraldo Editions

YGRG14X: reading with the single hand V

Dorota Gawęda & Eglė Kulbokaitė

07.06.2017 –

22.07.2017

Cell Project Space
258 Cambridge Heath Road
London E2 9DA
cellprojects.org

hunderstorm photographed by Anne Tetzlaff

THE BLOCK

theblock.art

IAAC

国际艺术评论奖

The 5th International Awards
for Art Criticism 2018

Entries Now Open

FIRST PRIZE 10,000EURO
3 SECOND PLACE AWARDS OF 3,500EURO

WRITERS AT ANY STAGE OF THEIR CAREERS ARE INVITED TO
SUBMIT CRITICAL WRITING IN CHINESE OR ENGLISH TO THE
INTERNATIONAL AWARDS FOR ART CRITICISM 2018
WWW.IAAC-M21.COM

ZABLUDOWICZ
COLLECTION
Invites

Guy Oliver
21 JUNE–12 AUGUST

Josefine Reisch
20 SEPTEMBER–28 OCTOBER

zabludowiczcollection.com

176 Prince of Wales Road
London NW5 3PT
Thursday–Sunday, 12–6pm
FREE ENTRY